FEUD AT SWEETWATER CREEK

FEUD AT SWEETWATER CREEK

A Novel of the Old West

by

Ardath Mayhar

Writing as "Frank Cannon"

The Borgo Press
An Imprint of Wildside Press

MMVII

CONTENTS

FOREWORD

When I first began writing westerns, I was determined to avoid as many *clichés* of the genre as I could manage. First of all, I knew that families were extremely important to everyone, no matter what the historical era involved, and writing a western story without taking into consideration the effects of the plots on the families involved was illogical.

I knew from family history, as well as a wide reading in journals and other contemporary records, that the women who went west were not the wimpy or whorish sorts depicted in all too many novels and movies. I wanted to show real people dealing inventively and bravely with unusual and interesting challenges. In each of these three books I feel that I may, to some extent, have succeeded in reaching some of those goals.

—Ardath Mayhar (Frank Cannon)
Chireno, Texas
September 2006

PROLOGUE

They came from many places: Washington, D.C., of course. Baltimore. Chicago. Even Denver, new as that raw city was. They met at the home of a senator whose name everyone knew, and they kept that meeting a secret.

"Here is the overlay we've prepared," said the timber baron. "We are claiming large blocks of land as we lay out the railway lines. This will give us control of access to the tracks and the towns that must and will grow up along them."

The eight large men moved forward to stare at the map and its overlay. They kept their poker faces, as always, but their eyes were greedy in their well-fed faces. *Land.* That was the secret of power, and they all knew it. The coal baron looked at the Rocky Mountains. "My scouts tell me there is coal there in abundance," he mused.

The man known in Chicago as Mr. Beef grunted. "Coal, timber, those're penny-ante things. Look at that grassland...miles and miles and thousands of miles of it. We can control the beef industry for the entire country...even the world!—with the grazing lands pretty much in our hands and the shipping totally under our domination."

The senator grunted. "Not easy. Congress is beginning to look pretty closely at the things we bring up these days."

"Then we must have no objections...by anyone. Either here in the East or out there in the cattle country. There are people who specialize in dealing with such things. I've used one several times for minor affairs of this sort. Fenchurch, his name is. A big fellow, British. He can stare down any suspicion he encounters. He can deal with any problems we find, from Missouri to the Rockies." Mr. Beef was grinning now, his obsidian eyes gleaming as if they had been oiled.

* * * * * * *

The horse was huge. Its head was as big as a trunk, and its belly was elephantine. It was dwarfed, however, by the man on its back.

The man who was known as Garvin, though that was not his name, rode along the indistinct trail leading westward toward the Sweetwater. Sleet stung his huge round face, making its paleness blossom with patches of scarlet. The scarf wrapped about his chin did little to keep out the cold of the winter storm.

Anyone else would have grumbled at being sent out in such weather. Not Garvin. He loved his work, loved the opportunity to dominate people, to hurt and even to kill them. That was why he was so good at his job.

* * * * * * *

Otis Elliot glared down at the letter in his hand. He looked up at the man who had brought it from town as if trying to find a way to blame him for the contents of the communication. "Damn!" he said, with much feeling.

"What's the matter, boss? Something gone wrong?"

Elliot was not reticent about his business—not with those involved in bringing it to fruition.

"They're sending in another man...what they call a specialist in difficult cases! After I've got rid of everybody in this valley except just those fools down there on the creek...you'd think they'd appreciate how hard it is to scare these people. They're not your eastern types, easy to intimidate. And now they tell me I'm not working fast enough to suit them.

"Congress is getting ready to consider some new legislation...hmmm. Looks bad, if we don't get this finished off pretty soon. We have maybe two years to get everybody out of the valley." He looked up again. He was thinking hard, frowning a bit.

"Some of those homesteaders have got kids. That gives us a handle on those families. If we scare a couple...even kill one or two, if it takes it...that'll send their folks skitting back east so fast their heels will burn." He focused on the ranch-hand's face.

Jim looked shocked. "Kids?" he asked, his tone as shocked as his expression. "I never hurt no kid in my life!"

"Then you can get, right now," said Elliot. "I don't need any weak-bellied sissies on this spread. We've got work to do. Important work that's going to benefit this entire country when it's done. What's

11

a kid or two when it comes to making this the strongest country on the face of the globe?"

Jim backed away. "I'll git my stuff," he said. "I got no call to go changin' the world. Not at my age. You git somebody else to go killin' kids for you."

The man left the house, and Otis stepped to the window, to watch him making for the bunkhouse. When he had disappeared he went to the kitchen and called, "Les! I need you!"

A redheaded man came yawning from a side room. "Boss? You need somethin'?"

"See that old fool doesn't get to town," he said. "He might shoot off his mouth to somebody, and even if the marshal does have his orders from upstairs, he isn't a bit happy about this situation. I can tell. We don't want anybody around asking awkward questions, do we?"

Les grinned sleepily. "Guess not, iffen you say so, Mr. Elliot. You want me to get him now?"

"No, you idiot! Wait till he gets away from the Sweetwater all the way. Out in the middle of no place in particular, that's the place to drop him. Hide his body, if you can manage to. Bring back his horse and gear. We can always use those."

When Les had left, Otis Elliot went back into his study. He looked thoughtful. Getting rid of Jim was a good step, he thought. This new man the railroad people were sending in should appreciate somebody with the decisiveness to get rid of weak links.

Garvin—never heard the name before that he could recall. He wondered what sort of fellow he was. A specialist at this sort of business? The thought made Elliot shiver.

FEUD AT SWEETWATER CREEK, BY ARDATH MAYHAR

He would hate to be in the shoes of all those Fitches and their kinfolks down there along the creek.

FEUD AT SWEETWATER CREEK, BY ARDATH MAYHAR

CHAPTER ONE

Fitch came out of the draw at twilight, and he came cautiously. Behind him, across the long stretch of dry lowlands, the sun had set, and he felt confident that even the Apache, whom he had seen crossing the skyline at noon, wouldn't be able to locate him easily. Not that he had any qualms about mixing it with any Apache ever born, but now he had good reason to want to live to see the end of his journey.

He didn't stop at once, for he knew that the edges of the forest were ahead, and he much preferred to shelter among the scrubby junipers and piñons. Steady and patient, he guided Outlaw up the imperceptible slope that led, eventually, into the mountains. The critter was tired, as he was himself, and there was time to take time. Hurrying wasn't his way, for he had learned very early in his thirty-year lifespan that letting your impatience run away with you could get you killed. He had seen so many kids during the war, all fire and fury, dash into battles and ambushes and forays and come out as bundles of blood and guts. That had never been his way.

Now the forest loomed ahead, blacker against the darkness and faintly outlined in stars. He dis-

15

mounted again and led Outlaw, stepping softly and leading the horse over the softest ground his booted feet could locate. They gained the trees, and he stood for a long time, holding the horse's nose so he wouldn't make any sound and listening to everything he could perceive in the woods. Since the war, the whites and the reds were head to head, and he had no intention of stumbling into the middle of a fight that wasn't his own. He had enough of that coming up, he figured.

Now the duff from the pines muffled his steps, and he went on into the deeps of the woods, finding his way by instinct, for it was blacker than black. But the long years of scouting and soldiering and acting as guide had given him a few more senses than the average white man, and he moved as an Indian would have, finding a camping spot against a low bluff of stone. He built no fire, but just unsaddled Outlaw and watered the beast in his hat, dug out a double handful of grain for his nosebag to make up for the lack of grass, and set his back against the rock. With his blanket carefully wrapped so as to leave his limbs untrammeled, he leaned his head back against the chilly stone.

He had slept very little since getting that letter in his pocket. Some primitive urge had driven him, with his usual clock-like steadiness, across the desert country, eastward toward his father's small spread in northern New Mexico. He had been so sure that his family was safe and well-found, even with all four sons gone. They had worked all their young lives beside Pa, digging a good well to build the house over so that water would always be available, no matter what. Breaking the watered land in the little valley for corn and vegetables; buying,

16

trading for, and raising a likely herd of cattle to range the empty grasslands that swept from can to can't across the wide country.

And once the three cousins had moved out from Mississippi to join the Fitches, homesteading spreads up and down the Sweetwater, he had felt confident that they would be all right. He and his brothers had gone off to war as happily as if they had good sense. The Confederacy had lost, anyway, and Mark and Frank and Johno were dead. George Fitch had never forgiven himself for being so gullible.

Now he was going home, and he knew with bitter guilt that it was long past time. Like so many of his fellows, he had drifted, after the war, into soldiering in the West, then, as his skills made themselves known, into scouting. The years had rolled past without much to mark one from another—until the letter had come, finding its way more by the mercy of Providence than by any plan of man.

He needed no light to read it. It had been read until the paper was fragile and the copperplate writing almost illegible.

Dear Son,

Your father and I dislike calling upon you, for we know that you have made your own life, now. However, there is trouble here that we are unable to deal with, alone as we are. The Sweetwater Valley has become a place of danger and harassment for all of our family who settled here when it was empty even of Indians.

17

Your cousin Robin has been murdered as he worked his herd along the high pastures. His wife and children gave up the place and returned to Connecticut, where Martha's family is still, praise be to God, living. Harold Nations, your cousin Etta's husband, was so badly wounded from ambush that they were forced to give up and return to East Texas, where his people live. That leaves only John Fitch and his wife and seven small children, and they are getting terribly uneasy, for the children have been threatened.

Who, you may ask, is creating these problems? I am ashamed to tell you, for it is my own cousin, Otis Elliot, who moved here the year after the war ended. At first, he settled in, worked his land and built his home, and cooperated quite well with the rest of us. Then things changed.

I cannot tell you how or why he has entered upon his present plan of action, but it will, I'm certain, have to do with money. He has always been overly fond of the idea of wealth and power, and now he has found someone who is backing him with money and armed men. His home has become a fortress, guarded round the clock by blackguards.

Your father and I traveled up creek to see if we could resolve whatever problem there might be, after the first indication of trouble (Robin was shot at, but that time the bushwhacker missed). We were surrounded by his henchmen a full mile from the house, and they escorted us the rest of the way, watching us as if we were desperadoes.

Otis was sitting behind a desk half the size of the Mississippi farm, and he was nobody I ever knew. Something has changed him into a hard, calculating grabber. He let us know in no uncertain terms that all of the family would be forced out of the valley, willy or nilly. There was no offer to buy our land, just, "Get out or you'll go out feet first."

You can imagine how your father took that. Ab stood, rocked back on his heels, you know how he does when he is angry and controlling his temper, and he told Otis, "We Fitches don't scare worth a damn, Elliot. You'll have to kill us, every one, and you'll know you've been in a fight. I don't know who or what's behind you, but however it is, it's going to cost more money and blood than most people are willing to pay."

I remember every word as if it were etched on my brain. They were the last words he has been able to say clearly. Otis's men escorted us back almost to the main track, and then they opened up on us. God alone saved me, and I grabbed the reins when Ab dropped them. The mare was scared out of her wits and took off at top speed. Ab was down on the floor in front of the seat, not making a sound, and I was sure he was dead, and I almost turned and took after them with the rifle. The mare wouldn't turn, though, and I think the men were ashamed to hunt down an old woman like me.

When we got home, I found your father was alive, and he still is, but he can't walk and can hardly talk. I think the John Fitches are about to give up the fight, now, and without them, I will be the only able-bodied person left to stand against Otis. Make no mistake, I will stand until I fall, but I need help. Old Tildy is still with me, and she's a feisty old soul, but she's over eighty, now. Her spirit is willing, but she can hardly lift the big shotgun. We share watches, she and I.

I am hanging on, hoping that God will send this letter into your hands. I am sending it out by the peddler who comes every year. He said he would do his best to send it toward your last address.

Perhaps the army can find a way to get it to you. If you can come, Son, we need you badly.

Your loving mother,

Kate Fitch

George reckoned that God had had a hand in it, sure enough, for the letter had come into the hands of Sergeant Baile, who had kept track of his old drinking buddy. Baile had only had to wait six months to pass it on to him, which made it less than a year since the letter had set out from Sweetwater Valley. What might have happened in that time, George didn't like to think, but he wasn't one to borrow trouble. He was on his way, and nothing but death could stop him.

Fitch shifted quietly against the rock, listening to the wind in the treetops. Here at the edges of the mountains, snow could come unexpectedly, even this far into the spring, and he felt in his bones that the weather was on the change. Snow would slow him, and he must cross this range and a lot of country beyond before he reached his destination.

It was beyond his control. Tonight, he must rest. Fitch turned off his thoughts with a conscious act of will, and sleep overtook him.

Outlaw woke him before dawn. The hobbled gelding, knowing his master's habits, stood beside him, a blacker bulk against the dark treetops, as Fitch opened his eyes. In ten minutes, they were on their way, and no trace of their stay marked the spot in the forest behind them where they had rested. Even Outlaw's droppings had been hunted out by Fitch's keen nose and buried beneath the pine straw. At this point, he figured he didn't need any Indians to complicate his life.

The country grew steeper, and they were in the foothills. The trees were thicker, now, and taller, and it was slow going, without any trail. Fitch, however, knew in his bones that the Apache were still on the trail he coveted. When his inner warning system stopped whispering to him, he would cut across to catch the track. Until then, he would struggle through the country as he was. A man lived longer if he listened to his hunches, he had found.

Before noon, he came over a roll of hill and saw before him a cupped valley, clear of forest, where the tender spring grass made a green glade. Knowing that Outlaw needed to rest, Fitch circled the clear spot until he found an arm of woods that extended into it. There he dismounted, loosened the bit, and let Outlaw crop the grass that had edged into the woods as far as the sunlight allowed it to.

The man sat against a tree, munching jerky and sipping from his water bottle. In these mountains water was fairly plentiful, but his long habit of getting by on as little as possible made him abstinent. His eyes, always alert, wandered across the glade, peering intently into the edges of the trees all about it. On the far side of the clearing, he could see something that was neither grass nor dirt. Something brownish and grayish. He kept coming back to it, not staring steadily, for that could make the eyes see motion where none was, but for a few seconds at a time. And it moved. Not much, but it definitely moved.

Silently, he rose and *tchk'd* to Outlaw. The horse raised its head, looked at him reproachfully, and followed without being led, as Fitch slipped around the edge of the clearing to the spot nearest the moving thing in the grass. With another pains-

22

taking scan of the surrounding area, he stooped his long, thin frame and flitted out into the open.

When he dropped to his knees beside the gray-brown lump, he found himself looking into a pair of black eyes that, reasonable or not, were calm and quizzical and filled with amusement. They were set into a face so tracked and darkened by time that the old man it belonged to seemed mummy-like. However, the toothless jaws moved.

"Took you plenty long," the old Indian observed. Fitch gaped down at the spread-eagled figure. Then a grin slowly creased his weather-beaten face. He distrusted heroics and dramatics, but sheer toughness combined with humor got him every time. He busied himself cutting the thongs that tied the thin wrists and ankles to stakes that had been pounded into the ground.

"Who might you be?" he asked, helping the Indian to sit up. "And who staked you out?"

"I be Tracks Through the Air," the animated mummy said, flexing fingers and moving feet, though it was obvious they were extremely painful.

"Come from east—I Cherokee. I come to Apache with message. They not like my words. Too old to be danger they think, so they leave me here. I know you come. Tracks Through the Air sees ahead."

Without leaning on Fitch, the ancient made for the forest, hobbling badly but making good time, nevertheless. "Not good to stay in open, here. Apache come here to hunt in spring. You got food?"

Fitch took out a strip of jerky, looked at the toothless gums, and shook his head. "This is mighty tough going, even with teeth," he observed.

Tracks Through the Air grinned. "Been gum jerky a long time. Need water, too. Long time out there, no water. Mouth dry."

Fitch offered the canteen, and the old man sipped sparingly, then set his mind to the jerky. Somehow, he managed to masticate it and get it down. When that was done, he looked slightly more like a living being than he had before.

"Better go," he observed, looking at the sky over the clearing. "Snow coming, pretty soon. You go east...not want to be snowed in here. Come."

And to Fitch's amusement, the oldster began hobbling up the slope toward the notch that lay hidden in the forest far above them. George caught Outlaw, slipped the bit between his teeth again, and mounted. Coming up beside the Indian, he reached down.

"Might as well ride," he said. "You don't weigh enough to give this horse any trouble. We'll make better time."

Tracks Through the Air caught the proffered hand and was lifted onto Outlaw's rump with so little effort that Fitch found himself trying to decide exactly how much the old fellow did weigh. About eighty pounds, soaking wet, he thought. Mostly gristle and guts.

Fitch had known many Indians in his career. Those he had scouted with had been a mixed batch, some whiskey-hounds, some sober and reliable men. They had kept mostly to themselves, even on scout, but he had never disliked a man simply because he was a redskin. He'd killed plenty of them, make no mistake, but they'd been earnestly trying to do the same to him, and he never held grudges on account of war. As for his new traveling companion, he found himself liking the little guy. There was a spark of humor in him that touched a sympathetic chord in the depth of his own character.

As they climbed, they could get a better view of the sky, for the trees here were very tall and stood well apart, leaving clear avenues between their boles. Woolly windrows of clouds lay low, and the feel of snow was in the air. "If we were on the trail," Fitch grumbled, "I could take us right to a good deep cave. Be just right to spend the night. We could have a fire, even, because it curves back, a way inside, to hide the light. I'd surely like a plate of bacon and beans. Figure you could do with something hot, too."

Tracks's dry voice floated up over his shoulder. "Apache there tonight. Just as well we not on trail. I know other place, just as good. Camped there on my way. When you see big rock in hillside, stick out like sore thumb, stop. I show you then."

Outlaw climbed steadily, either carrying the two or following Fitch as he went ahead. Tracks's weight wasn't enough to burden the beast. Before dark, the snow began to fall, lightly at first, then more heavily, the big, light flakes settling and melting, then sticking to the needles of the trees and the juttings of stone from the soil. The "big rock...stick out like sore thumb" was capped with white by the time they reached it, and they were seeing by snow-light, for darkness had fallen.

Sitting atop the tall horse, Tracks looked about. Hunched in his thin shirt and scarred leggings, he looked too frail to retain anything so heavy as a memory, but his eyes moved expertly across the slight ridge that anchored the rock. Then he pointed off to the right, behind the outcrop. Fitch walked

25

ahead through the thickening snow, rounded the rock, and saw a spot of deeper blackness looming in the groin that joined it to the greater outcrop, which the obvious one hid from view.

"Good place," said Tracks, dropping from the horse's rump and staggering toward the opening that caused the dark blot. "Just in time. Not young as used to be."

Panting, the old man sank onto his haunches, just inside the low cavern that twisted off to the right, seeming to lead downward. "Spot for fire, fifteen paces in. Big crack let smoke go out." The wispy voice fell silent, and Fitch hurried his attentions to Outlaw, tethering the gelding, supplied with his nosebag, in the shelter of the angle between the stones.

Dumping his packs, he felt about in the darkness until he laid his hand on the Indian. Only by the hiss of breath did he know that the old man still lived, and he struck a match and looked about. It was a likely spot for a night like this, and he grubbed his candle end from the pack and lit it, then went out into the snow for fuel.

He had a fire going quickly and lifted the old man onto one of his blankets beside its grateful glow. His small iron pot went into the edge of the coals, filled with snow and jerky, for Fitch felt that hot broth would put new life into the tough old bird.

And it did. After gulping a couple of tin cups of the stuff, Tracks Through the Air sat up and demanded something solid for his gums to work on, and Fitch gladly handed him some of the leathery jerky. Bacon and beans followed, washed down with coffee so strong it should have melted the pot.

Both of them felt better, then, and they sat in warm lethargy, recuperating from their day.

In a bit, Fitch went to look out into the night. The wind was blowing, now, and the snow was streaking sideways through the trees, drifting high against their northwest sides. He made his way back to the fire, laid the end of a good-sized log in it, and stretched out in his other blanket.

"May take a while," he said.

Tracks nodded. "Two days," he said. "Then we go."

Fitch didn't believe in foreseeing prophets, and he hadn't any reason to believe the Indian knew what he was talking about. But the thing inside him that attended to hunches had a feeling that maybe, just maybe, he did. A prophet could be a hell of a handy thing to have around on the errand he was about.

"How you manage to be where you were?" he asked Tracks, who didn't move.

"Tell you tomorrow," he said. "Going to be a long day, anyhow. Make shorter, tell tales."

Fitch laughed for the first time since he had received his mother's letter. Tomorrow, indeed! Then he fell asleep.

CHAPTER TWO

When Fitch peered from the cavern the next morning, it was hard to tell that it was day at all. Dark clouds hung low overhead, and the wind-whipped snow made the forest an anonymous blur five paces from the portal. Outlaw huddled in his sheltered spot, and Fitch unfolded the saddle blanket and spread it over his back to keep off the worst of the cold, though he knew that the hardy gelding didn't really need it. Another nosebag of grain (now becoming scarce in its cloth bag) settled the horse down to dreamy munching.

When he returned to the glowing heap of coals, he found Tracks Through the Air building up a fire with some of the wood gathered into the shelter the night before. Without speaking, the two set snow to melt, made coffee, then sat, one on either side of the blaze, sipping from tin cup and tin can. It had been a long time since Fitch had found someone who didn't need to fill up every minute with talk, and he savored the silence, companionable and undemanding.

There wasn't anything to do when the coffee was finished except sit and stare into the coals. Fitch had had so little time in his active life that the pastime soon palled on him. He broke the stillness himself. "Said you'd tell me a tale come today. Might use up some of this time."

Tracks grinned. The firelight and shadow turned his wrinkled face into a demon mask as his cheeks stretched wide. "Good time make talk. Tracks Through the Air tell many tale. This time...plenty time. Make long story. All right?" His dark eyes sparkled as a stick of wood broke, throwing up a spew of bright flecks.

"Long time ago...much before white men so many...Tracks Through the Air was medicine chief. Look to sky, look to land, look to trees and plants for know things." He poked at the fire with a dried branch, his eyes seemingly focused inside himself, seeing that distant past.

"Sang song over many sick, many wounded. Often they get better. Some die, of course, but many live who not expect to. Old men respect me. Young men envy me. Long time, now. Too long...." He sighed and shifted his position so as to look directly into Fitch's eyes.

Those bright eyes were full of many alien matters that George shivered to think of. But the old man smiled and went on with his tale.

"Have three wives. Many sons, many daughters...all strong and some bright. Life good, then. Hunting very good...we live like animals in forest...like deer or bear, never thinking ahead. Tomorrow very far away. Streams full of fish, woods of game...we happy, sometime.

"Whites come, by and by, and settle nearby. We not worry...plenty of land, plenty of food for all, we think." He laughed, a harsh chuckle without any real humor in it.

"Not know then that never is enough for white man. All there is, too little for him. More than is, still too little. Time go by. We begin to have trouble. White man push into our hunting lands. Kill all game, laugh when we go hungry.

"I dream, then. Dream say, 'Go away from white man. Go to west, where forest has no end. Get away from trouble, now while young and strong and tribe has no sickness.' I go to old men in Council, say to them, 'We must get away from whites. Death come. War come. Sickness come, if we not go'." He stared down into the licking flames.

"Old men ache in bones. Now I know why they not want to travel, but then I very angry. Still, they no say for tribe to go. Say white man new in country, not know ways. Say whites get better when settle down." The bark of laughter came again.

"White man *never* settle down. Get more and more, push into hunting grounds, push into cornfields, push into village. Miss'naries come, tell us we wrong. About everything. Wrong gods. Wrong life. Wrong work. Must do their way. I tell chiefs again.

"They look...still much game. Still much land. No war...yet. They tell me go cure sick people, not warn chiefs like silly old woman."

Tracks spat into the flames, which sizzled angrily. "I go away, then, but something talk to me. Say big trouble come soon. Much suffering, much death. I try again to talk to chiefs, but they not listen at all.

"I take my women, four sons, six daughters, all things we need to live. We go west." He sighed, remembering. "Forest go long, long way west of lands we knew. We see many trees we not know, many

30

animal we never see before. Already whites there, some build cabin, some plow field, some even build town. We stay away from all whites for long time. Then oldest wife get very sick."

Fitch leaned forward to put another chunk of wood on the fire. "Bad business," he said.

Tracks Through the Air nodded. "Very bad. She lung-sick, you know? Cough, get weak. So I go to white man town, near big river. Ask for place to stay while wife get better. I work to pay for white-man medicine, for my medicine too weak for this sickness. I say this to woman at big house. She say we stay in little house. She give medicine."

The fire sputtered loudly, driving damp from the fresh wood, and the old man poked it again with a stick. "She good woman. Her family good people. We stay there. Oldest wife die, but still we stay, help in fields, help hunt, fish for family. She teach me many thing. Teach some children read white man's writing. Teach wife many thing, too, about care for sick people. We like that place, those people. But old father die. Woman marry...and new man not like Indian. We almost forget, in that long time, where we start out to go, but now we pack up weapons, blankets, start over again.

"Big river hard to cross. No white man much on other side, but plenty Indian. We stay on river bank, build hut, live there for long time. New baby come. Oldest son killed by bear. But we grow corn, hunt, fish in river. Life is good again. Time pass and time pass, and white man come again."

"Can't get away from 'em," said George, remembering his own efforts after the war. "There's just too many of us, and that's a fact."

Tracks sighed. "True. We must go again. Steal raft from white man, go across river with horse. Stole him, too." He grinned. "Go into more big woods, find Caddo people, big lake, small river. They welcome us. We settle there for long time. Almost forget white woman, all she teach us. But remember some thing and that help make good medicine for new people.

"Life good there. Live long time...get old there." He fell silent, lifted the canteen and sipped a little water.

Fitch said, "You knew what they were going to do to your people? Take their land...send them away?"

"Not for long time," said the cracked and grating voice. "Dream not say what. Just say go. We go. We learn many thing we never learn with own people. Learn many thing we not like, too."

Fitch grunted meditatively. If the old fellow was telling the truth, and he had no reason to doubt him, then he just might have some sort of handle on the future.

"So what sent you away from the Caddo?" he asked.

"Both old wife die, young wife run away. All sons like Caddo, not my people. And white men come again. Make big boat, take whites across river into land of Tejas. Caddo pushed and pushed. I warn them, same like old chiefs. They not listen, same like old chiefs. Too old to argue with them. I go to Territory, find my people again. This time they listen to Tracks Through the Air. Trail of Tears teach 'em much."

The old man stared into the fire, his face a mask. Fitch leaned forward and pushed a chunk of wood deeper into the flames.

"How come you don't hate me? I'm white. My kind has dealt your kind a lot of misery."

Tracks Through the Air nodded. "Did hate, for long time. Angry fit to kill. Then voice tell me, 'Every man different. Most Cherokee stupid, back in old lands. You not stupid. Most whites push and take. Some whites not. Every man different. Not hate all because of some.' So I think and think. Old age cool down blood, head run things more. So I try to teach my people. Be smart, I tell 'em. Not get pushed in corner. They try, but not much good.

"Young ones finally think to join Apache. I tell 'em Apache not much better than whites, but they go, anyway. Long time after, I go after to find what happen to them. Apache laugh and stake me out, and there I am till you come. Voice say you come. Say, 'Jorfitch come up mountain. Be here soon. Hang on, old medicine chief'."

Fitch started. "My name is George Fitch," he said. "They told you my name? My God!" He was certain that no mention of his name had passed his lips. Unless the Indian could read English—through a shirt pocket and mackinaw—there was no way he could know it.

Tracks Through the Air grinned secretly into the fire. Huddled in the blanket, almost touching the nearest coals, he seemed to drift off into a dream, leaving Fitch to ponder on his story. Nothing could take his mind from his own problem for very long, though, and the lean man spent a long day either dozing or worrying. Before dark, he went out and walked back and forth through the woods. The snow had stopped, and the wind died down a bit. In winter, he knew, bitter cold would have followed, crusting the snow. This far into spring, he was not surprised to find that it was a bit warmer than it had been. The white layer was knee deep, but soft—even a bit slushy in spots.

He went back into the cave and told Tracks, "Looks as if we might make it out tomorrow, if it doesn't freeze too hard tonight. It's pretty mild, considering."

The Indian shook his grizzled head. "Long 'bout midnight, cold wind come. Freeze slush so slick horse break legs, man break neck. Two days we be here. Sit down and drink coffee I make."

George sat and poured coffee into his tin cup. Something inside told him that it would more than likely be another day before he could take up his trek. Tracks was, for some strange reason, very convincing.

"I've got to get home fast," he said to the air. "There's trouble, and it may be even worse now than it was when Ma wrote the letter to me. She's holding off a white land-grabber all by herself. Pa's crippled, and the old Negress is so little and frail a good breeze could carry her off." Something about putting the thought into words eased his inner tension.

Tracks raised his eyes from the fire and looked into Fitch's. "We get there soon. I know good ways. Came with Paiute, partway. He show me trails nobody use, passes nobody know. He old hunter, all alone. Tribe throw him out, wife throw him out. He spend life wandering mountains, crossing flat country. He show me much, tell me more. Try to steal medicine pouch from me, and I kill him." He sighed, as if regretting the untrustworthiness of people.

"Whoa," Fitch said. "Who said anything about taking you with me? I can put you on the road home when we get down the mountains. Somebody will be going your way. I've got to travel fast and light. It's been almost a year since Ma wrote, and there's no telling what has happened since. She needs me there day before yesterday."

"I go anyway," the Indian said. "You take me with you, you get there fast. You go alone, by white man's roads, you get there too late. I think on you last night. I dream on you.

"Somebody wait on main road. Wait for you six seven months, now. You be bushwhacked, you no trouble. You get home, you big trouble. See white woman...tall woman, strong like man. She wait, too. Shoot in night, work in day. About wore out, seems like. Barn burn; she build another, all alone. Some woman!" He cackled admiringly.

"You mean you saw my mother in your dream? And you saw somebody waiting to ambush me? You know, Tracks, I'm not used to people who can see things they *can't* see, if you take my meaning."

"You wait. Get used to it. You brighter than Cherokee and Caddo. They not listen, they lose their pants! You listen, you maybe live a while. We go together. Voices say do that."

"But what about your people? They need you, seems to me. Don't you need to get back to them?"

Tracks's guttural "ho-ho-ho!" rumbled through the cave. Then he said, "They glad to see me go. I ask question, they got no answer. I make 'em think; they no want to think, not at all! Be glad I never show up again."

35

Fitch sighed, then said carefully, "But light as you are, Outlaw can't carry double forever without wearing out. We've got a lot of rough country to cover, and I haven't enough money to buy an extra horse and weapons for you. I'm going to stock up on ammunition just before I get home so I won't have to carry so much weight a long distance, and that'll just about clean me out of cash. I left before they had time to pay me for my last job."

Tracks's eyes glittered. He fumbled at his throat and drew forth a lumpy and odoriferous skin bag that hung from a thong about his neck. "Apache scared of pouch." He grinned. "Strong medicine. They know; their medicine chief know. Not touch. Got many kinds of magic things. Got gold, too. Whites not know other magic, just gold."

He dug into the pouch with two fingers and drew out six double eagles. "This buy horse, pistol, good sharp knife," he said. "Maybe horse not so good, but it got four legs, can carry me."

Fitch laughed, and the sound boomed about the curving walls. A thin rattle of gravel trickled down the wall at his back, dislodged by the vibrations.

"All right, you old devil. You can go with me. Right now, I'm not so certain you won't be a lot of help, too. You sure we can leave soon?"

"Two mornings," the old man answered. "Then we go. Tomorrow, you tell me all story. About letter. About land. Pass the time." He closed his eyes and fell into a doze, even as he spoke. Fitch shook his head. Here he was, now, saddled with an old medicine man so thin-boned and fragile that a good gallop might break him like a handful of twigs. Going into some sort of bloody setup alone was pretty dumb. Going into it with Tracks looked to be just plumb foolish.

Still, that spot where his hunches lived said nothing against it. In fact, he felt strangely comfortable with the situation. Putting the whole thing out of his mind, he set about preparing a meal. One good one a day was about all they could afford, stuck here as they were, and he had been looking forward all day to a hot supper. While the coffee was boiling, he went out again.

The forest was still and white, the snow still soft underfoot. Outlaw welcomed a handful of oats, and Fitch scuffed around the little clearing about the rocks until he uncovered a fair amount of dead grass. Outlaw whickered, and the man rubbed the soft nose. For the past few years, the gelding had been the only steady friend he had, and he enjoyed a few minutes of communion with the beast.

Then his hunch-maker rose up in alarm. He knew, sure as fate, the forest held some enemy, and that enemy was more likely than not Apache. He raised his head and sniffed. Wherever the crack in the roof led into the air, it must be much higher that this spot. There was no tang of smoke to betray them. Only Outlaw gave tangible evidence that someone was sheltering in the cave.

The opening was not terribly large, but he thought he could fit the horse through it, with effort. He closed his hand about Outlaw's nose, signaling silence, and led the animal toward the dark spot that was the entrance. When they started inside, the beast resisted trying to pull sideways, but the narrow opening frustrated him. With a soft scrape of hoof against rock, they were through, and the horse stood nervously as Fitch hissed at the sleeping Indian, "Apache in the woods!"

While the horse was led into the tumble of stones that filled the back end of the cavern, Tracks covered over the fire, first rescuing the coffeepot. "You see 'em?" he whispered.

"No. Just felt like they were there," Fitch replied, checking his loads by touch. "You think they might be making for this place?"

"Could be, Apache know their country. Hunting party in snow, maybe."

Fitch crept into the first part of the cave, just inside the opening. Finding a spot behind a low knee of rock, he settled himself so that his feet wouldn't go to sleep. He laid both pistols on top of the protrusion and leaned his rifle against it, all ready to hand. It was still faintly light outside, and anyone entering the cave would be blinded for a bit in the darkness.

He sniffed. A faint aroma of coffee lingered in the air. He only hoped that chilled noses would take a moment to identify the scent. A split second was all he needed.

There was no sound, but he was suddenly aware that Tracks was just behind him. "This time, maybe not have to kill," he breathed into Fitch's ear. "I think whites out there. Maybe guide with them. Good whites, bad whites...maybe we wait and see?"

Fitch exhaled carefully. "Maybe...." His voice was less than a breath on the still air. His hands didn't move away from the guns. A dull squeak of snow underfoot could now be heard. Maybe two sets of feet. Not many. The pale irregularity of the opening was obscure, as a dark shape peered into the cave. An explosive cough shattered the stillness, and a plaintive voice said, "Herb, if there's a b'ar in there, you'll have him all waked up an' mad."

"Knowed this here cave for ten years; an' there's never been a b'ar here yit," a big voice boomed. "Injuns, mebbe. Rattlesnakes in summer, but who needs a cave in the summertime? No b'ars!"

"Then haul your freight on in, 'fore we freeze," the other said.

"Somethin' pekoolyar, here," the booming voice said. "Seems like I smell somethin'."

"You couldn't smell your upper lip with that cold you been packin'. Come on, let's get our stuff inside and build a fire. Got melted snow down my boots, and my feet are about to freeze off!"

Fitch inhaled slowly, then let the breath go joyfully. He knew both voices and their owners were, if not friends, at least friendly acquaintances. Herb Yardley and Pincus Wills hunted and trapped and hauled freight and guided greenhorns, as they found the opportunity. Neither was overly bright, but they were pretty good men in a fight, and neither was known for being a thief or a bushwhacker.

"Don't get rattled, boys," he said, his voice quiet. "You've got company this time that isn't a bear or a rattlesnake. Come on in. We've got a fire that we can put back together in a couple of shakes, and there's some coffee mighty near boiled. I just hope you killed some fresh meat today. That'd go down good with beans and hoecake."

"I be damned!" said Herb. "That sounds like Fitch, the army scout. That you, George?"

"Right. You got horses?"

"Well, it's a long story. We *had* horses, to begin with, but a bunch of Apach' shot 'em out from un-

39

der us. Mighty near shot *us* out from under us. We just barely scraped out with our packs and guns. Had some meat, but I guess them red devils're roastin' it right now. We got a little honey, though, for our hoecakes."

By this time, Fitch had the fire flickering again, and the newcomers sank onto their heels to survey the situation. When their eyes fell upon Tracks Through the Air, they looked at Fitch inquiringly.

"This is my friend Tracks Through the Air. Cherokee. You can thank this gent that you didn't get shot when you stuck your head in the door. He told me you were white, else I'd likely let you have it. We been avoiding those same Apache you ran into."

Herb looked at Pincus, who looked solemnly back. Then both turned to the wizened medicine chief. "Happy to know you, Tracks," drawled Pincus. "Much obliged for savin' our necks. Guess we owe you somethin'."

Tracks grinned his demonic grin, the fire dancing on his wrinkles. "Might be, you pay back. Pretty soon." And with that enigmatic statement, he fell silent.

Beans and hoecake soon filled the cave with good smells of food, and the four made good use of the honey Pincus had stolen from a bee tree some weeks before. But all the time they ate, the two newcomers kept looking sideways at Tracks Through the Air. When the last belch had sounded fruitily, they turned their gazes toward the old Indian.

"You kind of got my curiosity riled up," said Herb.

Pink nodded agreement. "What did you mean, we may pay back?"

Tracks grinned. "I think you got troubles. I think you not able to trap again soon, mebbeso. I think you need thing to do, maybe pay, maybe not, but keep busy, all right?"

The pair looked at each other. They turned to look at Fitch, who kept his face poker straight.

Pincus leaned forward onto his elbows, bringing his face down to the level of the old man's. "Now how in hell did you know that? Maybe we have had a few problems. Maybe we can't pay old Fergus down at the trading post. But how did *you* know about that?"

Herb interrupted, his big face furrowed with lines of unaccustomed thought. "We do have troubles, Pink. And we cain't pay Fergus. Don't make no difference how the old feller knows...."

Fitch leaned forward to stir the fire and move the coffeepot deeper into a bed of coals. He looked up at Wills. "What did happen to you two? Besides the Apache, I mean?" he asked.

The little man sighed gustily. He settled back as if for a long story. "What didn't happen to us?" he asked.

"Well, George, you know how Herb 'n' me works. One year we may haul freight for one of the companies. Take turns drivin' and ridin' shotgun, which works out real good. Or we may guide some bigwig out of the East who wants to shoot a griz out in the mountains. For what, we've never found out."

Herb broke into a deep chuckle. "Tell 'em 'bout the last one o' them, Pink. The Mighty Hunter! That's a tale worth the tellin' on a snowy day!"

The smaller man's narrow face split into a grin.
"'Tis, for a fact. This businessman come tootlin' off
the train someplace back around St. Louis. Hires
him a guide who don't know his tail from a hole in
the ground and starts out west to shoot him a big
bear. He rides the stage to Santa Fe and hops off
with that tame guide of his right into the arms of
Skinner Brady."

George began to smile. The smile got broader
and broader until he, too, was chuckling. "Who
skint him good and proper, I'd guess."

"No doubt of that," Pink agreed. "But once he
understood he'd been rooked on horses an' equipment, he had to straighten things out. He was one of
them that has more'n one set of skins. Sent for more
money, got the marshal to look up old Skinner.
Cussed a whole lot and drank a little while he
waited for more money."

"We was between jobs, right then," broke in
Herb. "Met him in the bar...Lucy's—you 'member,
George?—and got to talkin' to him. Told him we
knowed the mountains like our mamas' faces, which
ain't no lie at all. Told him we knowed where there
was a grizzly so big he could stomp a mountain flat.
And that maybe wasn't the entire truth, but it wasn't
no total lie, neither."

"No way," said Pink, shaking his head. "That
bear is big enough to handle a catamount with one
paw and a bull moose with the other."

"You knew where he ranged?" asked George.
"And led that eastern dude right up to him?"

"Well not to say it was that direct. We parlayed
some, got him up to a price we liked. Then we all
waited for his money to come by the wire. Though I
never did understand how they could git gold to

travel over that little bit of stuff...seems like magic to me."

George looked down hastily to hide his amusement. Beside him, he could feel Tracks shaking with silent laughter.

"Anyway," the little man continued, "the gold finally come, and we checked out the equipment old Skinner had skunt him for. Some we could use, some we had to start over with. Sold the horses to a family of Injuns who wanted to eat 'em. They wasn't no use for anything else.

"We took off for the high country, and that dude sloshed all over a saddle like water in a bucket. Never thought, back East when he decided to go huntin', about not havin' hansom cabs or railway trains runnin' right up to where he wanted to go. Time we got up really high, he wasn't breathing too good, either. When we told him we was goin' to walk the last handful of miles, I thought he was goin' to croak."

"He was pretty game, though, Pink. You got to give him that," said Herb. "He kept up fairly well, considerin' he was wearin' fancy ridin' boots all the way."

"Till we found that bear," said Pink, his tone wry. "Herb was rangin' around lookin' for the critter, and Clemmons and me was goin' right straight up the trail...or as straight as you kin go up that trail...and when he come runnin' back, yellin' that he'd found Old Bloody Bones, it was the first time in all my life I ever seen a feller turn snow white an' faint dead away."

"Well, that was 'cause Old Bloody Bones'd decided to foller me back an' see who was comin' to call on him!" objected Herb.

"I didn't see you wastin' no time gettin' up that tree," said Pink. "You passed me on the way up, I'll swear to that."

"You left your...client...lyin' on the ground?" asked George. "Did he survive that trip, or did you bury what was left?"

"Oh, he didn't come to no harm at all. That damn bear looked up at us fer a while as if he could wish us out of that tree. Then he run back to where Clemmons was lyin' and begun sniffin' around him. Clemmons come to once...I seen him open his eyes, but the bear was sniffing his collarbone, right about then, and off he went agin. It was the strangest thing, George. That critter sniffed him all over. Tried to turn him over an' sniff his back, too. Looked around him, tried to git into his pockets. You'd of thought he was a New York pickpocket, the way he done.

"Then, after a long time when Herb and me was just about to fall outen the tree we was so tired and sleepy and hungry, Old Bloody Bones just up and took off up the trail agin. Never saw no more of him a'tall."

"And what about your Easterner?" asked George. "Was he satisfied with his hunt?"

Herb broke into a guffaw. "Told us he was satisfied to've saw the biggest damn bear in the world. Said he wouldn't've shot it if he'd been awake, 'cause he wouldn't ever have been able to decide where to start shootin' it. Like shootin' a mountain, it would've been. He paid us a bonus an' headed back East on the first stage."

"But that don't tell you where we been this season," said Pink. "We trapped this year. Got our stuff from Fergus, as we usually do. Went up and trapped all winter and done real well. Had a load of otter an' beaver. A couple of foxes would make you weep they was so nice. Plenty to pay off Fergus an' set us up for the summer, so's we wouldn't have to stir a peg till next fall.

"Now we still owe Fergus. All our furs're gone, along with the traps an' the horses and all our grub and stuff. Them Apache just stole us down to our skins, just about. An' Fergus ain't goin' to stake us to no more till we kin pay him some on our old bill."

Tracks grunted. Fitch looked at him, shriveled and wispy in the firelight, and understood exactly what he was proposing.

"Now, Tracks, I see what you're getting at, but how in hell can we manage mounts for 'em, when we just barely can manage some sort of hack for you?"

The trappers looked from one to the other, puzzled. "Hey, now, what you talkin' about? Where you wantin' us to go that we'd need horses so bad an' so quick?" Herb asked.

"I've got trouble at home," Fitch said. "Bad trouble, and nobody who goes with me may be able to come back. You likely won't want to get yourselves into it, anyway. Looks like it's just going to be me and my ma and old Tracks here, up against a whole bunch of hard-cases. Already run most of my family out of their valley. Just Ma left; Pa's been shot all to hell, and Cousin John is scared for his kids. Probably gone, by now. So it's just Ma and old Tildy, that can hardly lift a shotgun any more."

Herb's eyes lit up. "A rip-snortin', honest-to-goodness fight? Man, you don't know what you're sayin'. We been lookin' for jist that kind o' fight

45

ever since the war. Bunch of damn carpetbaggers done took my pap's little old patch of sandy land away from him, an' they kilt him a'doin' it. Iffen there'd been anybody left to fight for, I'd've give 'em a fit, but I didn't want to stay aroun' Georgia, no way. You kin count me in, for shore."

He turned to Wills. "What about you, Pink? You in?"

The skinny little man nodded. "Might's well. No point lettin' you get in over your head, like you always do. One thing, though. How far we got to go?"

"Clear across the tip end of the Sangre de Cristos, over to the country south of Ratón," Fitch answered. "And I appreciate the offer, I mightily do. But how in hell can we scrounge up enough horses to carry us? It's a long way, gents."

"Those Apache got plenty horses," Tracks said dreamily. "Been takin' horses all spring. I see horses with cavalry brand, horses with many other brand. They steal mighty good horses. We steal 'em back."

The three whites sat still in the firelight, mulling over his words. "You said we couldn't travel until day after tomorrow," Fitch said, finally.

"No weather for travel. Plenty fine for steal horses," he replied.

CHAPTER THREE

It wasn't the most peaceful night George Fitch had ever spent. While he was an old hand at Apache trouble, he had never gone looking for it since his army days. It went against all his instincts; bad as stirring up a hornet's nest with a stick. Of course, he decided at last, if hornets had kept horses, it might have been a little different, too.

Herb and Pink hadn't seemed at all upset. The fact that their own mounts were in the bunch tickled them mightily, and they went to sleep amid grunts of silent laughter. And then they snored until the cave echoed. Fitch could have stood the Apache problem. He turned back into the cave and toed the two trappers awake.

"Let's go, boys. Apache aren't going to expect trouble on a morning like this. We can get to the cave on the trail long before first light and hit 'em while they're still groggy."

"Kin we eat first!" rumbled Herb, standing to stretch his awesome length.

Pink snorted. "You kin be so damn dumb. No, we can't eat first. They'll be up an' around pretty soon, as it is. Get your gear and come on!"

"You stay here with Outlaw, Tracks," Fitch said to the Indian. "It's too cold to get your bones out in this weather...."

"I know good way to hide trail," the old man observed. "You bring horses right back here, might as well bring Apache right along, too. Crust too light. Won't hold up horse. Paiute show me place along trail, just right for us."

"Then I guess you go," Fitch said, wondering wearily how he had somehow lost control of the situation.

It was eerie, traveling over the crusted snow in the ghostly light. On the steep slopes, they stepped carefully, hoping that their moccasins, hastily cobbled from the hides they all carried for ground sheets, would grip and hold. Even at that, Herb slipped once and tobogganed downslope until a young pine stopped his slide.

It was easy to go silently. The cold was so intense that the world seemed frozen, their own breathing seeming the only thing to be heard. And once they sighted the trail, they warmed to their task, sinking into the crust and working their way forward, parallel to the track.

Fitch, who had traveled the road many times, knew exactly when to cut into the forest in order to come around from above and behind the Apaches' shelter. The faintest tang of smoke was in the air, and he sniffed and nodded. "Still there," he said.

Tracks Through the Air hissed through his teeth, "I stay here. You bring horses uphill. Hard to do...they not think you do that. Then I show you where to go. Can't tell. Must show."

Fitch nodded. He motioned for the others to huddle close, then he said, "I'll go down and tend to

48

the scouts. There'll be some, at least, with the horses, and likely one uphill, just below us here. Maybe more. You hear me whistle, real low, you can close in. Stay a good way behind me until then."

Then, without a word, he eased down the slope, keeping low, his bowie knife in his teeth. There was a low ridge a hundred yards above the cave, and he worked his way along it cautiously. Then he eased one eye's width over. Sure enough, the Apache scout had used its shelter to hold a bit of warmth for himself in the icy darkness. The man was outlined darkly against the snow below him as he huddled against a rock.

There was a faint *whick,* and the knife sank to its hilt in the scout's back. Fitch was there almost as quickly, catching the man's neck in the crook of an elbow to stifle any cry. But there had been none. The Apache had died between one breath and the next.

Knowing that Herb and Wills would be behind him, George bellied down the slope, which now eased somewhat as it neared the formation that held the cavern. He was sure that the horses would be bunched in the small glade on the other side of the trail. He had put his own mount there more than once in bad weather. It was sheltered, and there was killed grass under the snow.

He ghosted across the trail, then froze to the ground, sensing his surroundings. There would be pickets with the horses, he felt certain, and he intended to stay put until he located them. Hands and feet numbing with inaction, he lay there, listening. But he smelled the first warrior, who was moving silently toward the trail behind him. Knowing that he'd be plainly visible against the snow, he rolled under a clump of bushes and waited. The man passed, and Fitch rose behind him and cut his throat. There had been little commotion. The scuffing of moccasined feet against the crust was about all. Still, Fitch welded himself to a tree trunk and waited again. There was nothing more for a very long time. A line of faint light showed beyond the treetops downslope. He decided to move, willy or nilly.

Easing around the perimeter of the glade, he came face to face with a startled youth, whose mouth opened for a yell as his hand came up with a knife. Fitch hit him in the Adam's apple, stilling the cry. Then he tangled with a desperate bobcat, who squirmed strongly in his grip. Only the fact that he outweighed the boy by at least forty pounds saved his life. Once he was able to roll on top of him for a moment, he got a good grip and broke his neck. The snap was sharp in the still air.

Their four mounts (they took an extra, in case of accidents) made a trail that any greenhorn could have followed, but Fitch worked them upward on the wrong side of the trail, sticking to thickly grown areas as much as he could. A fortunate overhang that had held the snow off the ground beneath led away in the right direction, and by dawn they stood again beside Tracks.

The old Indian had rolled himself in Fitch's extra blanket while waiting, but he was unrolled and ready for action by the time they reached him. He motioned southward, behind him. "We go fast, now. Not mind noise. They look for big bunch first. Figure they catch rest later. Then come after man who kill scouts." He scooted off ahead of them, and the three young men were hard put to keep up at all.

It was now daylight. The sun was rising, though a thick cloud cover hung just above the horizon, promising another gray day. Tracks was chasing madly across the treacherous crust, and Fitch had, more than once, to steady the two horses he was leading, not to mention saving his own footing by hanging onto their halters. The others, too, were doing a lot of thrashing and cursing. Up ahead, he saw that Tracks had paused and was waiting for them.

When they reached his side, they looked down in astonishment. Below them was an old watercourse. Its sides were so steep, the opening at the top so narrow, that no snow had accumulated. Only isolated pockets could be seen. The only problem that Fitch could see was the fact that the sheltered groove went roughly north and south, and they needed to go off at an angle.

Tracks jumped down into the groove and moved out of the way. "Come down!" he said, and Fitch shrugged and urged one of his pair toward the edge. It resisted him, but he managed to make it jump. After that, it was easier, and soon men and mounts stood in the sheltered tunnel.

"This is fine and dandy," Fitch said to Tracks, "but how do we get back to where we want to go?"

"Not worry. There's 'nother channel long a ways. Go right close. Better come fast, now. Apache pretty mad, I bet."

The bottom of the old stream bed was solid rock. Only leaves and needles from many autumns littered it, and they took little impression of hooves or feet. Evidently, this had been a strong underground stream that had, in some convulsion of the land, gone dry and been cracked open. Fitch suggested this to Tracks.

The old man was panting now, but he thought for awhile. Then he nodded. "Mebbeso. Paiute say go into black hole, back yonder. Could be, both caves same, too. You look on walls, see where water run long time."

They went on in silence, able to see clearly now, as the daylight grew stronger above their pathway. In an hour or less, they could see ahead of them a complication of the way.

"Other channel go off toward where we want," the Indian observed. His voice was a bit faint and unsteady, Fitch noticed, and he caught up to the hurrying figure.

"You ride awhile," he said, picking up the ridiculously light shape and setting it on one of the horses. "Hunker down so your head won't hit the overhang. You've done more than a day's work, I'd say. You got to remember that you're not a boy anymore."

"Long time, not boy," he replied. "Man get old, he stop, he die. Tracks Through the Air *never* stop."

"I'm not asking you to stop, just to ride for awhile. Keep your legs strong in case we have to do any running," Fitch answered. There was no word from the Indian, but George noticed that he didn't insist on getting down.

The groove they followed wound intricately, making it hard to keep directions firmly in mind. Now and again, Tracks would raise his head and look out over the lip of the stream bed to locate the now risen sun's pale dot beyond the clouds.

"More snow," he said at last. "Mebbeso we leave soon. Make food, pack up, go right off. Snow mebbe deep, this time. Make easy to go—crust get soft again. Not slide down mountain."

52

Then he rode in silence for a while longer. Suddenly, he raised his head and looked around. "This the place," he hissed. "Notch up ahead, horse can follow. Go right out on slope. Not far from cave."

Herb Yardley was in the lead, his huge hand holding down the head of the feisty mustang he had retrieved. It danced a bit as he pulled it into the narrow notch, but he gave a tug, and it followed him out of sight. Fitch went next, leading the extra horse, while Tracks rode his own pinto into the cut. When Pink joined them, moments later, they looked around to get their bearings.

"Damn!" said Herb, appreciatively. "Old Tracks brought us out right on top of where we wanted to go. Right down there is that knob of rock in front of the cave. I've come at the thing from every direction except this'un."

"We'll leave the horses right here in the notch," Fitch said. "Go back to the cave, grab a quick bite, pack up and light out. I'm not easy about all those mad Apache loose in these woods. They're the sharpest things on feet in the desert, and I'm not going to bet they're any worse off in a forest. Let's move before the snow flies, so it'll cover our trail."

When the four put their minds to it, they could move with amazing speed. In less than a half hour, they were on their way, three of them riding bareback on the skittish ponies. That wasn't the easiest thing in the world, considering that they were now going upward at a considerable slant.

"Wish't I hadn't cut up my buffalo robe for moccasins," said Herb morosely, as they paused to breathe the beasts.

"If you didn't have such big feet, it wouldn't of took the whole entire robe," Pink answered.

"'Course, on this grade, you'd slide right off an' on down to meet the Apach', did you have a robe on that wall-eyed mustang."

As they walked slowly upward, leading their mounts, big flakes began to fall lazily. "Good!" grunted Tracks. "Hide trail. Apache not think we go up. Easier to run away going down. Mebbeso we get away clean."

Fitch hoped so, but he wasn't near ready to bet on it. The way things were going, everything and its brother was going to get in the way of a speedy trip home. Though he had to admit that it was better to get there with four than with one, if it could be done. Sighing, he looked down the back trail. Their plowed-up trail was rapidly disappearing beneath the fat snowflakes.

He hated snow—had ever since the war. Seemed like that first winter he'd frozen stiff and never had thawed out properly since. The thought of the lower country ahead lent him new vigor.

"Come on, boys, step out. The sooner we get over this damn range, the sooner we'll be in the middle of spring again." He picked up his pack, and the others followed suit.

"Don't have to go over big pass," Tracks said. "'Nother pass, up ahead. Higher, mebbe, but come quicker, not likely Apache there. Come down, other side, very fast. Hit trail to Gallup. Very fast way to go."

Fitch looked at the old man, who staggered along stubbornly, leading his pinto. "Why in the world you want to get mixed up in all this?" he asked. "I'd have set you on your way back to Oklahoma Territory, seen you well found for the trip. You could go back and live in peace. Why in the world do you want to go smack dab into the middle of a fight that isn't yours, steal Apache horses, kill yourself walking through the snow? I just don't understand it."

The old man grinned, "Been medicine chief long time," he said. "Got no tribe that listen. Start new one. You, me, them, mebbeso your ma. Good tribe, no fools. Life get peaceful, Tracks Through the Air get tired living."

Herb guffawed. "Now that's jest the way I feel, Tracks. Gits dull, jest livin', with no fights to stir up the blood."

The Indian didn't answer, just pointed ahead. "Go steady, not break leg, mebbeso through pass tomorrow evening. Cold up there. Better camp early, rest up."

Nobody smiled. If the truth were known, Fitch thought, every one of them was worn to a nub already. Not only the old Indian needed a rest.

Chapter Four

They reached the shoulder of the mountain in a blinding snowstorm. The pass, off to the south of them someplace, was off-limits, probably watched by the Apache, so they followed Tracks's directions, climbing at a slant for hours, feet freezing, horses snuffling and groaning. The snow was piled deeply, layer on layer that had never melted all winter.

When they reached the downward slope at last, they seemed to be standing on the roof of the world. Lower mountains spread eastward, and in the distance they could see a white expanse that led to the lowlands curving around the foot of the Sangre de Cristos. The air was sharp enough to cut out a man's lungs, George thought.

Below and to the left George could see the line of white that marked the trail leading toward Albuquerque. "We can catch the trail when we get down there," he said to Tracks, who sat his pinto, huddled into his blanket.

"That will let us move fast. I'm not a bit easy about my ma. We need to hurry."

"Snow melt quick, down there," said the old man.

"Many good place for ambush—I come that way. You be sorry you take to main trail. Go cross country. Better so. Safer, quicker in long run."

George shook his head. "I know you think you can see the future, Tracks, but we need to make speed, now. You can see for miles, from here. Do you see anybody who could possibly be a threat? If we loop around the settlements, then back to the road, we'll be there a lot quicker than if we are too cautious and take the rough country."

The old man shook his head. His grizzled hair was full of snow, and his lined face looked pinched with the cold. "If you see 'em, they no danger to you. It's the ambushers you don't see make the trouble," he grumbled. But he clucked to his mount as George urged his own down the slope at an angle.

Pink and Herb had listened silently. Neither said a word as they followed, but George noted that both were watching everything, their heads moving back and forth, their eyes flicking toward any sudden sound.

They came into the lower country without mishap, other than a horse that stumbled and rolled— luckily when his rider was leading him instead of riding. To have escaped the Apache so easily seemed strange to Fitch. It made him a bit nervous. Such things couldn't be natural, he felt.

The snow, as Tracks had predicted, melted away under the sun of the next day, leaving the trail they were now following a morass of mud. They strung out along the edge of the track and rode steadily, resting the mounts faithfully but taking no extra time for themselves. Two small ranches loomed on the skyline, and both times they angled away into

the flatlands to avoid coming into contact with anyone who might betray their approach to Elliot.

Although George had intended to stop to replen-
ish his ammunition at one of the settlements along
the way, Tracks kept insisting that there was time
yet for that—that it was bad thinking to let himself
be recognized, even so far from his home. So they
went ahead doggedly, making the best time they
could manage.

They often cut around the long way, keeping
mountains between themselves and the trail, for as
they neared Albuquerque there were more travelers
on the road. The country rolled more and more
deeply, and that allowed less visibility, which eased
George's mind as they neared the Colorado. He angled off to catch a ford he knew that was passable
even in this time of runoff from the high snows.

There were cottonwoods growing along the
stream. He recalled that they were thick, big trees
with a lot of undergrowth. He kept watching Tracks
from the corner of his eye as they approached the
ford.

Less than a mile from the proposed crossing, the
old Indian looked up at him. There was a deep
wrinkle between his eyebrows. "Bad business, there,
George," he said. "You go there, you be very sorry."

"Ambush?" said Fitch. Tracks sighed and said
no more.

Fitch found himself arguing with himself. "I
don't really believe all this nonsense about seeing
the future," said one part of his mind. "But you listen to your hunches!" insisted the other. "That's different. This is...this is Injun foolishness. We're going to cross the Colorado and head for Santa Fe."

He looked back at Pink and Herb. "There she is, up ahead. We'll be across well before dark, and we can camp on the other side. If I remember right, there is plenty of good wood and shelter for us and the animals."

Wills glanced sideways at Tracks. "He sure seems to feel bad about this move," said the little man, his tone mild.

"I know, and I hate it, but if we go round to the only other ford that won't drown us, it will take at least an extra day. The water's at its highest right about now. The snow's been melting for days now... just look back at that last mountain. Nothing but a little old skullcap of snow left on the top. It's an unusually warm spring, this year."

"I'll go with you, George, don't worry. But I feel a little funny about it myself."

They rode silently for awhile, watching the line of cottonwoods draw nearer and nearer. They could hear, by the time they were half a mile away, the water growling among the trees, grinding stones along its bottom as the snow water fled down the country. Fitch found himself tense, listening hard for any sound other than that of the river.

"I think I'll wait behind that little knoll," said Herb. "Seems as if Tracks might be right this time, too. I just cain't seem to make myself ride right up to them trees, there. Iffen anything's the matter, I kin ride in as backup. Or else...I'll go ahead and you all kin wait to see do I make it all right. I ain't trying to get out of danger, mind you, but I hate to commit all our men at once, if there might be trouble ahead."

Fitch realized that he had the same feeling. He only insisted on doing this as a sort of rebellion against the thought of abiding by the prophecies of the old Indian.

"Good thinking," he said. "Why don't you and Tracks stay in that clump of scrub up ahead? Pink and I will go ahead as if we're just moseying along, unsuspecting. That just *looks* like an ambush up there, doesn't it?"

Tracks nodded, his eyes bright. Fitch and Wills kept their plodding pace toward the river, and the others melted into the scrub. It was twilight by the time the two rode into the first fringe of trees. Fitch felt his skin squinching up into goose pimples.

The river was now loud in their ears. The horses snorted and stepped up their pace, scenting the water. Fitch loosed his pistol in its holster and gave Outlaw his head. They rode to the water's edge, which was considerably above the usual waterline. The trees nearest the river were knee-deep in the swirling current. The ford, wide and flat, was completely hidden.

There was no sign of any presence except their own. Fitch rode right, Wills left, and they traced the line of the water for a quarter mile before turning back to meet at the track.

"False alarm," said Fitch, feeling foolish. "I knew I shouldn't pay attention to Indian superstitions, but something bothered me...."

"Don't feel bad," said Pink. "Me too. I was nervous as a whole passel of cats in a room full of rocking chairs. But there's nobody here. No ambush, no nothing. I guess we'll camp up in the dry, t'other side?"

"Might as well," Fitch replied. He rode back a way and raised a shrill whistle to bring in their companions.

They built a small fire in a sheltered spot to cook their beans and bacon, boil their coffee. All of them felt a bit foolish—except, perhaps, for Tracks. He didn't look at all sheepish. Fitch didn't say anything about the false alarm, and Tracks didn't mention his prediction.

They stood watch, but nothing happened. When the sky was light again they were getting ready to move, and Fitch rode out with dawn touching the eastern sky.

"We'll go southeast of Albuquerque, then cut north to Santa Fe. Looks as if there won't be any trouble along the way, and that will make our trip a lot faster and easier...." Before the words were fully spoken, a shot rang out. A slug spanged off a spur of rock just beyond Herb, and the big man ducked and spurred his mount forward and to one side.

"Down, you sons-a-bitches!" he shouted.

The others lost no time in obeying. A spatter of shots sounded in the dim light, and Fitch found himself crawling, snakelike, along the ground, pistol in hand, toward the spot from which that first shot had come. He'd seen the flash just as the crack had sounded.

He didn't worry about Pink and Herb. They were seasoned veterans. They'd be doing what was sensible and effective. Right now, he wanted to get the man who had shot first. There would not, he felt, be more than a handful. He was supposed to be coming alone, if he came at all.

He paused to peer around and through a thick clump of shrubbery. How had they known who he was? With three others, he might have been anyone. Unless—he glanced back at Outlaw. His mount had gone with him to the war, come back with him after.

61

He was getting very old for a horse, though he was still strong. His distinctive marking on his dark forehead—a long white blaze with a diagonal slash and star—might well have betrayed Outlaw's rider to the bushwhackers.

He could see something—perhaps a foot—move against the pale grass. There was a cluster of boulders beyond the bush where a dozen men might have hidden with ease. Fitch listened intently.

He heard a horse snort. He heard the clink of a spur against a rock, but that was behind him, and it was probably one of his own group. He heard... careful breathing. Beyond the rocks.

He backed quietly from his position and made for the other end of the cluster. His knees bruised themselves against small stones, and his hands ached with taking his weight on the rocky soil, but he made it without making a sound.

He pressed himself against the end boulder and risked an eye's width around the far edge. He could see a denim arm, part of a shoulder. He moved a bit farther. The man was watching the other end of the clump, pistol in hand. His hat concealed most of his head, and he was facing the other way.

Fitch could have back-shot him, but he could see his father's disapproving look as he thought it. He cleared his throat politely.

The man whirled on his knees, the gun coming up as he moved. Fitch's slug took him in the upper chest, and a blossom of blood spangled the denim jacket.

Someone was coming, walking hurriedly through the crackling brush. Fitch, in his turn, whirled, gun corning up, but he lowered it when he saw Tracks, moving with un-Indian carelessness in the noisy undergrowth.

"All right, Jorfitch. Others all dead. We get 'em right soon. They not think we all so quick." He grinned his toothless grin.

Fitch rose to his feet, feeling tiny tingles and aches where the stones had cut his knees. "I got this one, too. You were right, Tracks. I'm sorry I didn't believe you."

The old man shrugged. "Now you know," he said. "We go way around Santa Fe, mebbeso?"

Fitch nodded. "Way around. I don't want to have to waste time on such as this. I have more important things to do with my time."

They moved together back to rejoin Herb and Pink, who had appropriated the guns and ammunition of the bushwhackers and added them to the packhorse. They took up the trail again in silence, and when they sighted a rider, far ahead on a flat, they turned aside from the road and headed for the deserted country to the northeast of it.

They moved swiftly when they could, slowly when the country was too rough for fast going. It was harder to ford creeks away from the normal spots, but they kept to the untraveled ways.

They were well into the rolling country, now. The going was speedy, and they made the most of it until they worked their way into the wild country west of George's home.

George knew they needed more ammunition, more guns. They were going up against what sounded like a well-organized takeover of the Sweetwater Valley, and he knew the enemy would be well furnished with weaponry. Yet he didn't send one of his companions in to buy more at any of the small places they circled.

Only when he arrived at the place that must have been his unconscious destination did he realize what was happening. He was going to Trant's. Surely Mr. Trant and his wife Mattie would still be there, keeping their tiny store, greeting those who passed with open-hearted hospitality. And they would know exactly what was going on over on the Sweetwater.

They put in a hard couple of days, pushing the horses as much as they could without exhausting them. The mounts, as well as the men, seemed to have a new lease on life, for the spring was now coming on rapidly. Grass was springing up, and the wind was relatively warm. The snows behind them in the high country seemed like a dream.

George came at the store from due west. Trant had always kept a good stock of weaponry. They could stock up there, and that, with the stuff they had recovered from the bushwhackers, would be enough to wage a good-sized war.

The closer they came to his home, the tighter grew the knot in Fitch's belly. If he rode in to find his parents' bones mixed with ashes of their home, he knew he was likely to spill more blood than it was good to think on. But he tried to be hopeful as they came in sight of Trant's tiny huddle of store-home and corrals.

"This time it's safe to go in," Fitch said to Tracks as they pulled up beside the corral. "Might as well see how the wind blows. Trant may know something...probably will, in fact. I've known him, off and on, since I was a boy. I don't think he'd ever do anything shady."

The Indian looked at him, eyes hooded and unreadable. "Mebbeso," was all he would say, but Fitch felt obscurely comforted. He was certain Tracks would have told him if he had any bad feelings about this move.

The porch was about to fall down, he saw to his surprise, as he stepped onto it. Trant had always kept his place very spruce, he remembered. The door was half open to let in the freshness of the mild morning, and Fitch called out as he pushed it wider.

"Mr. Trant! Mrs. Trant! Anybody here?"

He stepped into the long room that combined store and small bar. The stock was scanty on the shelves, and there were very few bottles on the shelf along the back wall. The place was empty, but he heard steps approaching from the side door that led to the living quarters, which had been grafted onto the side and back of the building.

A shock of unkempt white hair was thrust around the door frame, then Mark Trant hurried into the room and caught George around the shoulders. "My boy, I'm mighty glad to see you! Didn't know whether we'd ever lay eyes on you again, Mattie and me. Mat! Come see who's here!"

Fitch held the smile on his face by sheer willpower when Mattie Trant came through the doorway. The trim, blooming woman he had last seen a dozen years ago had turned into a walking skeleton. Her olive skin was tracked with masses of wrinkles, and her color was clay-like. Death seemed to be peering over her shoulder. Pitying, he moved forward and hugged her gently.

"Miss Mattie!" he said. "I'm tickled to see you again."

"Don't try to fool me, George Fitch!" she said with something of her old lightness. "I know I'm dyin' on my feet, same as Mark knows it. Only regret I have is leavin' him all by himself when I'm gone. The kids...Sairy married an' went west, an' young Mark didn't come back from the war. Same as your three brothers. Seems like it took off all the best young'uns from around here. Not one but you has come home again. I reckon we know why you're here, too."

She sat down rather suddenly in the rocker beside the cracker barrel, and her husband bustled under the bar and brought out a black bottle, from which he dolloped liquid into a glass. She took it in one gulp and sat still, her color becoming a bit less deadly.

"You tell him, Mark. All about what's happenin' over to Sweetwater Creek. I'm not worth killin' with a stick."

"Sit down, sit down," Trant urged George. "Have a drink. I guess you can use one, even this early in the mornin'. I know you must've come a long way." He poured a shot into a clean glass, and Fitch sat there, apprehension crawling through his innards.

"Before you get started, I need...I need real bad...to know if my folks are still alive. And still on the place, too."

Trant nodded his head. "Your ma is standin' off a whole passel of hard cases over there. Only thing keeps her alive is the fact that Elliot can't get 'em to hit her all out. They've got a lot of respect for her, and they don't cotton to killin' women, anyway. Your pa is so crippled up he can't do much, but he's able to watch in the daytime, now. She sets him up at the front window with that old ten-gauge, and he does right well. I sneaked over to take 'em supplies last month, and they was still holdin' out then."

"You mean they can't get supplies in?"

Trant shook his head. "He's scared off everybody in the country. Killed old Dill Henry six months ago. Dill told him he'd bring stuff out to the Fitches as long as he could draw breath. Elliot had him killed on his next trip."

"But Mr. Trant, how come you take such a chance? With Miss Mattie in the shape she's in, it seems awfully risky. Not that I don't appreciate you taking the risk and the time. You're a true friend."

"Couldn't do less, boy. Your pa and ma helped me get my patch of land, loaned me tools and labor to get my buildings up, stood by us every way they could. I'd be kind of a low-down sucker if I didn't stand by them in this pinch. And Elliot doesn't know about me. I'm so far away and so small, and the main road has shifted south from here, so nobody much comes through anymore. I'm *real* careful, when I go. Mat would throw me out if I didn't go, too."

The knot had eased. Fitch drew a long breath and smiled at the two. "I've got to have shells for my shotgun—twelve-gauge. Cartridges for three rifles and six handguns. Another rifle with shells. Another Colt, with ammunition. I've got three friends outside. You mind if they come in?"

"Sure, bring 'em in. If they're goin' to help you out over yonder, then they're more than welcome." Trant lined up three more shot-glasses and put a slug in each. Herb and Pink took time for civilities, then they headed for the bar with a gleam in their eyes. Tracks, however, looked at the whiskey and grunted.

"Make me sleepy. You got soda pop?"

Trant laughed and found a bottle for the old Indian, and he swigged at it while he looked through the small stock of guns and ammunition. He found a rifle that seemed to suit him and brought it to the counter behind Mattie Trant, together with a good revolver and a pile of cartridge boxes. Fitch watched, intrigued, as the ancient looked shrewdly at the pile of goods, then laid two of his double eagles on the counter.

Trant totaled the stuff and nodded. "Got a little change comin', too. You know money better than most of your folks I've met."

Tracks grinned. "Know about anything magic. Gold white man's magic, so I learn."

Herb and Pink had a little money left in their pokes, and while they looked around and made their selections, Fitch went with Trant and his wife back into the living quarters, where they lifted Mattie onto the couch and covered her with a crocheted coverlet. She dozed off in a bit, and Fitch looked at Trant.

"Why is this thing over at Sweetwater going on?" he asked. "What's in it for Elliot? What's in it for his backers, whoever they are? Sure, it's pretty good land, but nothing out of the ordinary. Plenty of water, of course, but my God, the Sweetwater's a long creek, and it runs into the Canadian. Hardly anybody had settled along it when I left. Why can't they go somewhere else?"

Trant spoke quietly, not to wake his wife. "It's complicated, George. The railroad's behind this whole thing."

"The *railroad?*" Fitch looked startled. "Hell, the proposed route is *days* away from Pa's place."

"It's not that simple," Trant replied. "Seems as if the bigwigs back East have taken maps and drawn blocks on it. Everything in each block is to be railroad land, no matter whether it's already been homesteaded or not. Washington's backin' 'em all the way, naturally. Pockets've been lined all up and down the line. The territorial governor looks the other way. The marshals've been warned to steer clear of this kind of fuss.

"Your folks're not by themselves. We've had people come through here who were half wild, mad an' hurt an' shot all to pieces. Lost their land. Lost their kin, a lot of 'em. Run out of the places they worked like slaves to build up.

"I got to warn you, boy. You take on Elliot, and you're goin' to be alone. Them that set their heels is mostly either dead or gone. There's a few that hangs on like coyotes to Elliot's coattails, takin' his leavin's. Your ma an' pa, me'n Mat, an' old man Graham is about the only independents left in the whole area. I'll help where I can, but like you said before, I got Mat to think about. I'm too old and shaky to be much good in a stand-up fight, anyway."

Fitch reached across the couch and took his hand. "You just don't know how much it's helped me to find out what the deal is before I go into the middle of it. I see I'm going to have to figure out some pretty dirty ways of fighting, too. You got any dynamite, Mr. Trant?"

Trant's eyes crinkled at the corners. "I've got a couple of cases," he said. "Never had much call for it, but we dug a well a while back and hit rock. It ought be good, still. Got percussion caps, too, if you need 'em. I won't sell it to you. Say it's a donation to the cause. You get that rat's nest cleaned out so we can knock the governor off the pot, and this country'll fill up fast. That'll be good for all of us."

They went out to the shed beside the well and found the dynamite. It was bulky, but Fitch thought the spare horse could carry it without trouble. The caps were there, too, on a high shelf, and Trant put them in a separate bag to travel on another horse. He also dug out a box of small bolts and stuck them into the bag.

"Got these by mistake. Cost more to send 'em back than to keep 'em. Make mighty good shrapnel, if you need such a thing."

"Mr. Trant, if there ever was any debt you felt toward my family, you can consider it settled. And if—when!—I get things straightened out over at Sweetwater, I'm going to come back and help you get your place back in shape. Maybe Miss Mattie will make it, now that spring is here. You think?"

"I hope," answered the white-haired store-keeper, lifting a bag onto his shoulder and making for the store building. "All we can do, seems like, is hope. Now you've come, maybe there's some point to it."

By the time they reached the porch with their burdens, the others had decided on their own purchases. Trant all but bared his shelves of ammunition, and the three knew that he was charging them ridiculously low prices for the stuff. He shook his head when they remonstrated.

"If things go on like they are, I'll be out of business before Christmas, anyway. If this can help you change things for the better, it's a good investment."

So they rode away with more than they had hoped for, and a little money still jingled in their pockets, too. It was still early, and the sun was warm in their faces as they rode eastward at a rapid clip. The long swells rolled away behind them, and Fitch found his belly beginning to knot up again.

They nooned beside a spring run-off creek that emptied, further south, into the Sweetwater. Fitch had camped there many a time with his pa, waiting for game to come down to drink. While the horses grazed, he walked to the edge of the stream and looked eastward through the thin stand of cotton-woods.

There evidently was no more coming and going from Sweetwater westward. The trail, which he had traveled every year or so on his way with his pa to visit the Trants, had disappeared. The grass was unbroken, rippling in the light breeze as it ran away toward his home. That was good, he reckoned. Elliot likely wouldn't expect anything to come at him out of the west.

They spent a scant hour resting the horses. Then they lit out eastward again, hoping to make the valley just at twilight. As they neared the fertile valley that held the creek, the land rose to a fairly high ridge, crowned with a line of stunted trees.

"We'd better take it easy from here on," Fitch told his companions. "It's not unlikely that Elliot will have men posted all around his spread, just in case of trouble. I'll scout ahead up the ridge. You all spread out and ease up it in a long line. That way, if somebody gets the drop on one of us, the others'll get the drop on him. It's not but a mile down to the creek from here, and only about three miles to our place. We may want to ride down under this side of the ridge till we get nearer. I want to go see, anyway."

Herb grunted. "All right. We'll Injun up the slope. No use sittin' up on a horse like a big damned target at the fair."

As Fitch dismounted, he handed his reins to Tracks and took his rifle from its boot. Then he turned on his heel and set out for the crest of the ridge, bending as he reached the top. He lay on his belly and peered over.

The evening breeze shifted a drift of dust into his eyes, and he squinted them against it. Below him, a knot of cattle ambled along, pausing to graze now and again. Evidently they were on their way to water for their twilight drink. They made good cover, and he looked away southward, toward his family's spread. The curve of the creek, with the thick stands of willows and cottonwoods, cut off the view, as he had expected. He turned his eyes to the north, where Elliot must have homesteaded. Across the grassy valley and over another stand of cottonwood a lazy column of smoke rose from a chimney that couldn't be seen. Elliot's without a doubt. The cattle below him were branded with a Rocking E. He had a notion that most of them had been brand burned, for his family brand was the Rocking E. Dammit, the man was a cattle rustler, in addition to all his other faults.

There was nobody in sight, up or down the creek. No scent of tobacco smoke was on the air, either. He couldn't hear a cough or a sigh, though he lay there for a long time. Nevertheless, he decided that it would be far better not to bring his group over the lip of the ridge until he was well away from that column of kitchen smoke.

The light was all but gone when he rejoined the others. They had taken a look, found nothing amiss, and returned to Tracks to wait for him. Herb and Pink agreed that it would be better to come in as near his home as they could.

"Don't stir up no smoke till you're ready to scotch him," Herb rumbled, and Pink nodded.

"We was a tad too close to that smoke to make me purely comfortable," he said as they mounted and rode southward.

The sun was down behind the mountains that edged the sky with a low and jagged line. A spent moon hung low in the west and would, they knew, be down in a short time. It looked to be dark enough night to suit anybody who wanted to sneak in where they weren't wanted.

CHAPTER FIVE

The moon was down, but the sky was clear and brimming with stars. The stream reflected a faint and irregular glow as it ran, and that gave them a bit of help in following Fitch down to the water. He paused at the edge and cupped his hands about his mouth. The mournful cry of a whippoorwill fluttered through the night, and the sound of the axe stopped abruptly.

Fitch said nothing, but just stood waiting, while his companions let their mounts drink from the chill waters of the creek. He kept his eyes on the dark blur that was his home on the rise across the creek, and soon his watchfulness was rewarded with a spark of light. Not much, just a chink in a shutter's worth. That told him that his mother had understood his signal, and he led Outlaw into the stream.

Moving quietly, they crossed the water and found the pale dust of the path that led away up-slope toward the house. Fitch's feet knew every un-evenness in that track, and he forged ahead of the rest, impatient now that he was so near the end of his journey.

"George?" came a whisper from behind the corner of the woodshed that loomed before him.

"Ma!" he answered, just as softly. "You all right? Is Pa still...."

"He's alive. I think he's getting a mite stronger. He'll never walk, son, but he's making out to do better at talking. Come in...oh! You're not alone. Bring your friends in, too. I'll take care of the horses. Better put 'em in the barn so Elliot's men won't see 'em in the morning. They keep a close check on everything I do here."

Fitch growled a curse between his teeth as she took the reins from his hand.

Pink, behind him, said, "Ma'am, I'd be obliged if you'd let me tend the animals. Just p'int me at the barn. I know you want to lay eyes on your son, an' I know he's rightly anxious to see his pa. I reckon it's not a time for strangers to come bargin' in on the family. You jest go on in, an' we'll handle the horses. They need a tad of grain, if you got any to spare."

Kate Fitch clutched her son's hand very tightly as she said, "I thank you, sir. The barn's that black blob off to your left. The gate will be right in front of you, but so low you may bump yourself on it before you see it. And there's a bag of oats right inside. The lantern hangs on a peg on the right inside the door. I'd suggest shutting the door before you light it. You can pen the animals in the back part of the barn. There's a gate inside for that."

Fitch chuckled. "I found me a likely crew, Ma, in a sort of unlikely fashion. Come on in. I need to see Pa."

The door that she opened for him was a surprise. In place of the heavy timbers that he remembered, there was a thinner door—sheathed with some kind of metal strips. He ran his hand over it.

75

"What happened to the door, Ma?"

"They blew it to smithereens with dynamite," she said. "If it hadn't been so thick and so tough, we'd all have gone with it. As it was, it held off the blast, but it didn't make good toothpicks when all was said and done. I built this out of boards from the corral fence. Mark Trant brought me some old plow tools he hammered out flat to help make it stronger. He's been the one that made the difference since John Fitch took his folks back East."

"We stopped by there on our way in. Thought it'd be better to come from a direction nobody would expect me from. Tracks says they've got men posted to look for me on the main roads."

"I don't know who Tracks is, but I wouldn't be surprised if he did. That peddler is a good old fellow, but he talks a mile a minute, and I know he must've told somebody along the line that he took out a letter to you. That would have shaken Otis Elliot to his boot heels. He kept asking about you when your pa and I were there. Pretended to be concerned about you, but I figured, after the ambush, that he was worried about your war record."

"My war record? I haven't been back since. How could anybody know about it? I know better than to think you went bragging all over the place."

"Those two Oliphant boys went a few months after you left to join up. They joined the other side, you understand, and you evidently made a big impression on some of the Yankees you fought against. They came home full of tales about Ferocious Fitch. Not bitter, you understand. Just seemed like they admired you a lot."

"I'll be dad...gummed!" he said, feeling her eye on him.

There was a grunt from the parlor, and they went through the dim kitchen into the cheerful room where the lamp burned in the center of a marble-topped table. The huge man sitting in the rocker gripped the arms convulsively. Then he held out his hands to his son.

Fitch knelt beside him and hugged him around the shoulders. "Pa," he said, "I came as quick as I could. I wish, now, I had come right home after they mustered me out. It seemed like, somehow, I couldn't think of settling down yet. I didn't like soldiering that much, but it was what I was good at, so that's why I joined up again in Arizona. If I'd been here...."

"You...likely'd...be...dead," his father said, very slowly and carefully. His pale eyes, very like his son's, went over him critically. "You...look...beat," he concluded, when his examination was done.

"Came mighty fast, once I got Ma's letter," Fitch said. "And I didn't come alone. I brought three men with me. Funny thing, all the way around." And he proceeded to tell the story of Tracks, the two trappers, and the raid on the Apache horses.

"They're good men to have with you in a pinch," he concluded. "But I'll bet old Tracks is about ready to drop. He's never slowed us an inch. Never complained at all. But he's got to be seventy years old, if he's a day, and I know he's tired enough to drop."

"Mighty...big...help," Ab said. "Too...few...before."

"We brought in a lot of stuff, too. Mark Trant practically cleared his shelves to give us enough weapons and ammunition. Even dynamite. Could come in handy."

Ab nodded. Fitch saw that the effort of speaking had told on him. He patted his father's shoulder and went into the kitchen where Kate was stirring pancake batter in her old yellow bowl.

"Go call your friends in, George," she said. "I'll have something on the table in a jiffy. Short of meat, now, but there's plenty of flour—Mark brought me a barrel of it—and the garden is producing nicely. I know they're hungry and tired."

Herb and Pink entered the house apologetically. In the confined quarters, Herb seemed even bigger than he was, and Pink found himself feeling awkward too. Kate, however, had them washed up and sitting at the long board table before they quite knew what was happening.

Tracks was another matter. Fitch decided that he could walk, just as he was, into the White House in Washington, greet the president, and never turn a hair. He was as much at home in Kate's orderly house as he had been in the forest. However, it was plain to see that the journey had tired him severely. After taking one look at his dark, seamed face, Kate filled a plate and set it before him.

"If you want more, just say so," she said. "You look as if you could use it."

The old man grinned his demonic grin and tucked into the plate of pancakes, beans, squash, and onions. He managed most of the mountainous plateful before he gave up. "Mighty good, mebbeso," he said to Kate as she set a fresh glass of milk beside him. "Too full. Must sleep. All right?"

"I've put you all in the boys' room. There are four beds back there, if you don't mind cots. We built the bunks for the boys to save room, and all they need is shaking out and making up. Be ready in just a minute."

She bustled away, and Tracks looked up at Fitch, who stood beside his place. "Good woman, your ma. Very strong, very brave. Good cook. Like to meet your pa. Can do?"

Fitch said, "Sure. Thought you maybe were too tired tonight, but I know he wants to meet you all. Come on in the parlor."

The old Indian and the crippled man sized each other up swiftly without seeming to. Only because Fitch knew his father so well did he know that Tracks had been fully accepted, red skin or no. Ab's eyes crinkled at the corners, and he held out a big, square hand.

"Good...of...you...to...come," he said with effort. "Need...all...help...we...can...get."

Tracks Through the Air looked him in the eye, for even standing he was little taller than the level of the sitting giant. "Think we fight dirty, this time. All right?"

Ab grinned back at him and nodded. Then his head fell back against the chair cushion, and Fitch saw he was very pale.

"If you're ready I'll show you where to sleep," he told Tracks, who nodded and followed him back through the kitchen, down the short hallway to the room George had shared with his brothers. Herb and Pink joined them there and looked around with approval. "Need be, we could get out of either window or up the hall," Pink observed, checking the fastenings on the shutters. "Not that I think we need to worry tonight. Nobody knows we come in, I'd bet on it. What we gonna do tomorrow?"

Fitch, at the door, turned and said, "Let's wait and thrash that out in the morning. We're all dead beat, right now. Sleep on it. Then we'll talk."

Tired as they were, they slept like rocks while Kate and old Tildy took turns at watch. But Fitch was up before first light, and Tracks was just behind him as he made for the kitchen, where Kate was already building her cook fire.

Tildy sat in a low rocker shelling peas. A bowl of peeled potatoes sat on the floor beside her, and that made Fitch think of something.

"Pedro—he finally died?" he asked Tildy, and she nodded, her turban bobbing with the motion.

"That old dog, he be twenty, he still alive. Mean as sin, up to his las' breaf. One of Elliot's men shot him wid a shotgun a year back. Like to have los' his foot. Pedro, he died wid his teef stuck in de boot." She cackled with laughter, and Fitch knew that the old dog would have chosen to go in just that way, given the choice.

The others came straggling into the kitchen very soon. Fitch and Herb joined forces to carry Ab and his chair into the kitchen, so he could join in the planning, while Kate, frying the last of their bacon, watched her biscuits and joined in when she thought of something pertinent.

"I figure," Fitch began, "that it would be best to hit 'em before they even know we're here. Mark Trant told me there wasn't any use at all trying to get the law interested. The marshals have been ordered to turn a blind eye in this direction. That frees Elliot to do his worst, but it also frees us to do the same. I've been thinking all night, off and on when I wasn't asleep, and here's what I've come up with.

"First off, we've got to whittle down their numbers some. Pa and Tildy can't ride, and Ma has to stay here with them, so that only leaves three—four!—of us." (He had caught Tracks's quizzical eye on him.) "We've got to set up an ambush, and with that dynamite we ought to be able to rig up something that would take out a bunch of them at the same time. Of course, we've got to get Elliot himself. Without him, I figure the whole thing'll fall apart. Nobody else has any toehold here. But first we've got to thin out his guards. Mark told me that he has more guards, day and night, than you'd think anybody could use."

Kate, long turning fork in hand, came over to the table and tapped the fork against the sturdy boards. "I knew there was some reason we grew so many gourds last summer. Tildy got some seed from the peddler, and they made a hundred gourds, all sizes. We use some for dippers and some for bowls, but there must be fifty stored in the shed, waiting for a use to be found. You take some of that dynamite and a handful of those little bolts I saw in the box you brought in. Pour the bolts into the gourd, cut off the handle until you can work the dynamite down into it, plug it with mud around the neck, and seems to me you'd have a bomb that would scatter a lot of men at one time."

Fitch's face lit up. "Now you've got my head cranked up again, Ma. I know just how we can use bombs like that. Listen...."

By daylight, the four newcomers to Sweetwater Valley had retired to the barn, where they spent most of the day manufacturing their homemade engines of destruction. They kept the horses under

81

cover, too, feeding them well with hay left from the winter before, along with another ration of grain.

When the bombs were done and drying, Fitch drew his companions into a circle and began drawing maps into the dirt of the floor with a twig. Every curve of the creek, every contour of the land about it was etched into his memory, and he sketched everything he could think of into his map, from the locations of cattle trails to the depth of the creek at different points. By the time he finished, Herb and Pink and Tracks had a clear idea of the lay of the land, as well as relative distances. Fitch's years of soldiering and scouting had made him something of an expert at map-making. So it was that his "troops" found themselves able to fix their own positions and movements with some accuracy.

Though none came very near, they saw several bunches of riders that afternoon. One or another of them spent the rest of the daylight hours in the loft, from which the whole loop of the creek, much of the valley, and even a glimpse of the loop beyond the arm of trees could be seen. The first bunch of men Pink spotted, and they numbered six or seven. They seemed to be looking at the Fitch spread through glasses.

Later that day, Herb saw two on the near side of the creek. They were riding toward the house, but Kate yelled from inside the back door, "Don't come a step nearer. State your business and go!"

One of them moved as if to continue, but the other seemed to be arguing with him. A bullet from Kate's rifle sang over their heads, lending weight to the cautious man's argument, and they both turned and loped back the way they had come. A short while later, Kate and Tildy came out of the house,

Kate with the rifle and Tildy lugging the big shot-gun. They drove the few head of cattle that still bore the Rocking E brand into the fenced enclosure be-tween the other side of the house and the creek. While they were working, Herb saw yet another man, also with glasses, keeping watch from a knoll up-creek.

"They're gettin' ready for somethin'. I think we got here jest in time, George. Seems to be they been watchin' too close, too constant, jest to be keepin' tabs on a couple of women an' a cripple. We better move before daylight tomorrow," he said, looking about at the other three.

"Mebbeso they run out of time," said Tracks, his eyes squinted at the dusty light that trickled through the cracks in the floor of the loft. "Mebbeso, rail-road men got to get land right soon or not at all. You think?"

His inquiring glance at Fitch was met with a raised eyebrow. "I dunno," George answered. "You could be right. I don't know how this political chi-canery works, but I do know there's about to be an election back East. Could be they're about to lose some of their backers in Congress. Can't bank on that, though. Best we can hope for is that another batch won't come down on us when we get this one cleared out."

The sun was disappearing over the western ridge when a line of riders moved northward along the path on the other side of the creek. They studiously avoided looking toward the house, and Fitch saw that as suspicious. He was ready now for things to move, and the thought of the night of waiting ahead filled him with unease.

"Might be, we could hit 'em at night?" he half queried, as they sat waiting for darkness to hide their return to the house.

"Might be," said Pink, "if we knowed his setup. As 'tis, though, you don't even know the layout of the house. Miss Kate said she'd only been in it a couple of times before things went sour, and then never had a chance to see how it set. Better stick to things we know, an' ambushin' is somethin' we've all had lots of practice at."

"True," George sighed. "I guess I'm just antsy. I'd hate to get here just too late to save Ma from losing her home—or her life. If we had more hands, I'd think about hitting the big house, while our bait draws off most of the men. But with things as they are, it might spoil the entire thing. Guess I'll just have to grit my teeth and wait."

So they waited, while darkness came out of the rolling lands and hid the area. Then they moved quietly to the house where Kate had killed and fricasseed two chickens, made more biscuits, and cooked up a huge pot of peas flavored with sowbelly.

"Miss Kate," said Pink, on completing his meal, "how kin we wiggle tomorrow, when you load us down with good food till we cain't move?"

"Move faster with belly not growl," Tracks said in his dry way. "Move faster, too, go to bed quick, sleep long. No time to talk, now. Time to get ready."

He rose from the table and went back toward the bedroom, and the other two grinned their thanks and followed him. George, left with Kate, Tildy, and Ab, sat on the long bench that had helped wear out many a pair of pants in his youth, and looked at his family.

"Ma," he said, "if things go wrong tomorrow, it may leave you in worse shape even than you were to begin with. I worry."

"Don't," she replied, reaching across the table to take his calloused hand. "We have been just hanging on by a thread, waiting for you to come. We know you can't do the impossible, but now I don't care. Just as long as we hit Elliot where it hurts, I'll take anything that comes after. If I know there's nothing to wait for, I'll hit him myself. He won't expect that. Your pa and I and Tildy have lived together for a long time. We know what we can and will do. We may not live, but by God we'll make it known that we died!"

Fitch looked into her dark eyes. He squeezed her hand and forced a smile. "We're going to win," he said.

Chapter Six

At three o'clock in the morning, they slid out of the barn lot, leading horses with muffled hooves. On the rump of Tracks's pinto hung two lumpy bags, and in the pocket of his borrowed shirt were two stogies. The other men were dressed in all the dark-colored clothing they could scrounge.

Ghosting through the early-hour darkness, Fitch felt as if he had been carried back in time. The dull scufflings of the wrapped hooves, the tight knot of nervousness in his belly, the feel of other men behind him, tense and ready, were all reminiscent of those days during the war, when he had been, truly, Ferocious Fitch. Many such sorties had fallen to his lot, for his iron nerve and his fertile imagination could turn lost causes into successes. Not, he reflected, that it had done any good in the long run.

They crossed the creek and followed the path northward, toward Elliot's place. In several spots the path cut across through fairly heavy timber, where the creek looped far back toward the east. In the second such arm of woods, he moved back along the line until he was beside Tracks.

"You rather do your job from a tree or from horseback!" he whispered. "In a tree, you're pretty well pinned down if they get organized enough to go after you. On the pinto, you'd at least have mobility."

"You say true—not boy anymore. Not steady enough from pinto. Go into tree. You know good one?"

Fitch grunted, leading the pinto aside from the track. "If nobody's torn it down, there's a tree house right above you. Rise up a little and see if you can see it against the sky."

"Ha! Floor up in tree! Plenty good. I go!" And Tracks Through the Air rose to his feet on the pinto's back, gave a slight spring as Fitch held the horse steady, and a thump and a scramble told his companions that he had reached the platform safely.

"Come daylight, I watch close," came a whisper down from the skimpy branches.

Another patch of trees a half mile up creek was the place Fitch had picked for hiding the horses. He strung them on a picket rope in the old cavalry manner, so they could be unstrung in a hurry. Then he, Herb, and Pincus stole forward, well aside from the path, toward the fence that, according to Kate, bounded the southern edge of the Elliot spread.

Skirting it, the three circled to come at the house from behind, for there was nothing in that direction for too many miles to count. As they moved, they counted four men standing guard, much too carelessly, at the corners of the yard and fence around the house. Dots of red marked cigarettes of three of them, and the fourth was whistling between his teeth.

Old habits were taking over for all three of the stalkers. Without a word, Fitch nodded toward the eastern edge of the enclosure, and Herb was gone on silent feet to take out the guard at the far corner. Pink grinned in the starlight and eased toward the man who stood some hundred yards away at the northeastern corner, leaving Fitch to take the north-western position.

Fitch's man died soundlessly, his throat cut from behind. Fitch set his cigarette carefully on the corner post of the fence, and from a distance it seemed that the guard still stood there. A gurgle from his left marked the end of Pink's prey. Almost simultaneously, the whistler fell silent. Another short wait, then Herb floated into range, his bulk blotting out a big patch of sky. Behind him, streaks of paler color signaled approaching daylight, and the three turned toward the house—only to hear the back door open and several sets of boot heels clatter down the steps.

Again without words, the three changed direction, flitting through the yard like shadows. Then, with a triple rebel yell, they took out the last guard as they passed him on a dead run for the trees a quarter mile beyond.

They left confusion behind them. In the precious minutes it took to sort out what had occurred in the area of the house, they reached their horses and mounted.

Then they turned back toward the house and fired into the front windows, bringing a flurry of lead in return, though it was still too dark for the enemy's marksmanship to pose any threat. They made another sashay across, drawing more fire; then they heard horses coming from the rear of the place. With more whoops, they broke several more windows, waiting until the horsemen were well in sight.

They took out for the woods, lying low, Indian fashion, on the necks of their mounts. Behind them, hooves clattered across patches of creek gravel, and slugs began to whiz over their heads. They hit the second patch of woods yelling like Comanches. Then they were through, out of sight of their pursuers. Dismounting, they slipped into the trees and lay down.

The group behind them came through the trees in a bunch—a fatal mistake. Tracks's first "bomb" took down four horses and riders, and a mindless scream began to ring through the place. Their fellows hadn't time to look to their fallen comrades, for the second missile exploded among them in a hail of flying bolts and nuts. A third and fourth followed, and the little wood was filled with fumes and stinks and shrieks and the mournful screaming of horses.

Fitch and his two companions covered Tracks's retreat to his pony, but none of his victims was in any shape to mark his going. Of the dozen or so men who had pursued them, he figured that at least half were either dead or so badly injured that they would be no threat to anyone for a long time to come. They had whittled the odds a bit. Fourteen to three wasn't nearly as bad as twenty to three. Of course, he reminded himself, Tracks made four. A good sound fourth he was, too, if used well.

Now he joined them, sitting his pinto calmly. Behind him was one of the bags, still lumpy. "Think maybe save these. Plenty damage, just one bag."

Leaving the dreadful turmoil of the woods behind them, they swung wide from the trail, using the trees along the ridge to cover their movements in case anyone in the shambles behind them was noting their going. They headed down the creek, flanking the Fitch place and passing by on the distant slope.

It had been decided that they wouldn't show themselves plainly to be connected with Kate and Ab. Though Elliot would probably add up two and two fairly quickly, George felt that if the four of them used the empty John Fitch house as their headquarters, only approaching the home place after nightfall, it might add a bit to the confusion. By day, he intended for at least one of his group to cover his parents' home from high ground. Any retaliation Elliot might send toward them he intended to stop in its tracks.

"Better hide bombs," said Tracks as they rode up to the deserted house. "Not like to get shot in bag. Pinto go up. I go up. Not good. May need again...keep dry."

"We won't be in the house all that much. They may search it while we're gone. I think maybe the smokehouse would be best. It's tight and dry. I helped build it. And we can hang the bag up high. It's so dark in there nobody'll see it even if they should look." Fitch led the way around the porch, noting with sorrow that Carrie Fitch's beloved flowerbeds were overgrown and full of weeds. It brought home to him sharply the changes that Elliot had made in this valley, which had been so good a place for living.

He reached the small, square bulk of the smoke house and turned the peg. The door swung open with a doleful creak. The daylight flooded into the smoke-scented space.

"My God!" Fitch breathed.

What was left of a man hung from one of the hooks in the beams across the roof. Months—maybe as much as a year—of smoke had preserved him, somewhat, although his shredded face wasn't a good thing to see. The glint of teeth at one corner of the mouth made a grotesque grin, as if the corpse found the situation amusing.

"Who kin that be?" asked Herb at George's elbow. "Reckon it's your cousin'?"

"No. Ma said John and Carrie and the children all drove out together in the big wagon they came in. And Robin had been killed, already. He's buried in the family graveyard, Ma says. Etta and Harold went together, too. I don't have a clue who this could be. Guess I better look in his pockets."

He reached, with some reluctance, into a pocket of the ragged pants. The body swung a bit, and he took out his hand hastily.

As the thing moved, a glint of light starred the hand. Fitch looked down at a small silver ring on the little finger of the left hand.

"It's Sylvanus Graham!" he exclaimed. "Got to be. He got teased all his young life about being a sissy and wearing a ring. It was his ma's...his pa gave it to him when she died, and he wore it. I guess he wore it the rest of his life. Likely it was grown in so deep, and so small besides, that it wasn't worth taking off his body.

"Damn! Young Syl...and that leaves old Syl Graham left with nobody but his daughter Em. Bad doings. Mark Trant told me the Grahams are the only people left, besides my folks, who aren't part of Elliot's bunch."

"Going to bury him?" asked Pink, turning his gaze from the corpse.

"Not right now. Bad as it seems, if we hide the bag up above him, nobody who looks in here is going to notice anything but him. Don't you agree?"

Herb hawked and spat. "That's no lie. Tie it up there and let's shut the door. That stink has took away all my taste for the grub Miss Kate sent with us."

They proceeded to hitch the horses onto the front porch, letting them stomp around enough to leave a good batch of hoof marks. They built a fire in the hearth and scrubbed out the rusty iron pot that had been left on its hook on the crane. In a little, there was a mess of bacon and beans simmering in it, enough to give the house a lived-in smell again, at least, though they weren't really hungry as yet. They laid their bedrolls out and did their best to make the place look as if several men had camped there for a good while.

Then they ate their cold beans, packed up their gear again, leaving satisfactory smudges in the dust and litter of the floor, and led the horses still further down the creek into a thicket. There they wore out the day, with the learned patience of the old soldier. About four o'clock, a bunch of horsemen came warily down the path beside the creek. It was obvious that the lesson of the morning hadn't been lost on Elliot's remaining men, for they had their eyes peeled so sharply that the watchers in the thicket held their mounts' noses, to keep them from whickering, and stood like statues in the concealing brush.

Behind them, rising above the trees, a column of smoke boiled into the air. Fitch touched Herb's elbow and nodded silently toward the telltale billow, and the big man turned his head to look. He grinned and raised one eyebrow. Evidently their ruse had worked, so far. The riders were evidently looking down-creek for them now. As no gunshots had been heard from upstream, they felt sure that the searchers had avoided Kate's place. Pink was on watch there for the afternoon, and they knew he would have signaled to them if anything had taken place that called for their help.

The column passed slowly, and Fitch was able to assess its members. This time there were seven men. Two were very young—little more than boys—and wore their guns and their hats and even their coats in the unmistakable manner of the would-be gunslinger. As he didn't intend to do any facing-down with anybody, it didn't bother him at all. Shootouts were for fools.

There was a man among them who made Herb Yardley look middle sized. His hat would have held a good half-bushel of oats in its crown, Fitch figured, but his body was so mountainous that it dwarfed the big head. His mount was huge, too, heavy boned and strong to bear that weight. As George watched, he pushed back his hat and wiped his sleeve across his forehead. The great, pale face that this action revealed was somehow frightening. It held no expression at all.

Even from the distance, Fitch could see the paleness of his eyes—empty like the face. And the color of the man's skin was weird—a maggot color. He should have looked stupid. Most really huge men that George had met were slow and a bit dumb and pretty well without menace. Not this one. Across the quarter mile that separated them, he got the impression of overwhelming intelligence— intelligence and almost palpable danger. In spite of himself, he shuddered as the face turned to scrutinize the thicket in which Fitch was hiding.

Behind the big man rode a thin Mexican. Though he wore a sombrero that obscured his features, his figure was wiry and alert, and George decided that he was also one to watch. He sensed more danger in him than in both of the young men combined.

The last three in the group were those old-young hard cases he had seen many times in the past. Somewhere past thirty, they had left the sense of their lives back in the bloody dust of their younger days. Now, he knew, they were eking out the time between drunks and brawls with what seemed an easy job. They were just the sort to find the harassment of harmless people a profitable and pleasant way to earn their drinking money. Before someone gunned them down, they had a lot of meanness left in them.

He watched the column out of sight. Then he sighed and turned to Tracks. "D'you ever see anybody quite like that big fellow? He made a rabbit run over my grave. Something about him scares the hell out of me."

Tracks stared down the now empty track. "See kind before, once, twice. He crazy. Not dumb-crazy, cold-crazy. Plenty bad. Plenty dangerous. We not have easy time if he in charge. Better make two-three plans. He see through things, that one."

Herb let out a whoosh of breath. "Well, that makes me feel easier in my mind," he said. "Thought I was goin' loco there for a minute. That bozo ridin' the elephant jest plain skeered the ever-lovin' *pants* off me. Not 'cause he's so all-fired big, though he is that, for sure. Give me the same feelin' you get when you wake up in the night and move, an' a rattler gives you warnin' that he's sharin' your blanket. Sort of a pee-in-the-pants skeered."

Fitch chuckled very low. "That is precisely *it*," he said. "And I can't see that a man who has that kind of effect on three tough nuts like us is going to be just another hired hand. He's smart. It stuck out all over him, like quills on a porcupine. I'd bet a week's wages, if I had any wages, which I don't, that he's some sort of scout or spy for the railroad. Elliot may think he's just one of the help, but if I were the railroad, I'd put somebody to watch Helpful Otis. Crooked as they are, they know damn well that any man who'd murder his own kin for profit can't be trusted out of sight."

"How can anybody stay aroun' somethin' like that critter without feelin' in his bones what he is?" queried Herb, frowning. "It'd be like livin' in the same house with a polecat. No matter how quiet he keeps, you're goin' to know he's there, jest by his air."

"Ma says Otis is so full of Otis, he doesn't have room for anything else," Fitch answered. "She says once he got his nose full of the smell of money and power, he could stand on a skunk and never know it. I guess she's right, too, and Big John there proves it."

Tracks had been standing beside his pinto, listening. His eyes drifted shut for a moment; then he opened them and looked into Fitch's eyes. "Better go your place. Right now soon. Something come. Mebbeso bad, maybe not. Can't see. Get there quick. Cross over, other side creek. This side—something bad on it. Go now!"

Without hesitation, the two white men led out their mounts, and the three hurried, still afoot, across the stand of trees to the water's edge. There they mounted and urged the horses into the water.

Here the creek was fetlock deep for a good third of the way. Then, as they neared the big eddy that circled in the deep bend of the stream, it got deeper, until the horses were up to their hocks in the cold water. They didn't cut straight across the eddy, but even edging it was a nervous business until the sure-footed Outlaw found good solid pebbles under him again. When he surged out onto the farther shore, the others followed eagerly.

Fitch didn't dawdle. He hit for the ridge, and in ten minutes they were riding north along the scrubby-timbered slopes just beneath it. He held Outlaw to the fastest gait he could safely make on the uneven footing, and before long they passed above the now blazing John Fitch house. The smokehouse, he was glad to see, was far enough to the rear not to have caught.

Another half mile brought him to a thick arm of woods just south of his mother's home. There Pink had volunteered to take up guard duty, and George whistled three short notes of warning as they neared the hiding place. Wills emerged from his hidey-hole as they came within sight of the house.

"Mighty glad to see you boys," he drawled. "There's somethin' mighty odd goin' on t'other side of the creek. You don't happen to have a pair of glasses in your pack, do you, George? I'd purely like to know what it is."

Fitch stared, squint-eyed, up the distance toward the spot to which Pink pointed. Dust rose on the other side of the first arm of woods. The woods themselves shook as no breeze could have shaken them. Then the first shape came out of the near trees, and Fitch grunted. "They're running a bunch of cattle right down the other side of the creek. A whole BIG bunch. Look at the way they're tearing up that little stand of trees! They figure to shake out anybody who's hiding on that side; then they'll probably try to do the same over here."

"Could be, mebbeso," said Tracks, "They think Miss Kate be fooled. Hit her fast while she watch cattle. You think?"

Fitch looked at the old Indian with much respect. "I think!" he said.

CHAPTER SEVEN

By now, the sun had gone behind the trees on the western ridge. Long shadows striped the bush-dotted slope below them, and Fitch, after watching the surging mass of cattle for a moment or two, decided that the dust and the shadows together made enough cover for an attempt at reaching his mother's house.

"Find yourselves good positions," he said to the others, "and keep your eyes peeled. I don't want all of us penned up in the house and barn if they come at Ma. I do want to check on her, warn her what may happen. I'll be back pretty quick if I don't get shot going down."

Taking off his wide-brimmed hat, he tied it to the saddle, loosened the cinch, and slipped Outlaw's bit so he could graze. "There's a spot of grass right in the middle of this stand of trees—over to the left, there. You might put the horses there, tethered to stakes. We want to keep them out of sight as long as we can."

Then he slipped into the brush, crouched low, and began working his way toward the yard fence, some fifty yards below their position. When the brush thinned, he went onto his belly and slithered forward like a snake, his dark hair with its streaks of sun-bleach blending in well with the cover. Now and again he paused and peered through the grass-stems and bushes toward the melee on the other side of the creek. The cows were bawling and trampling, trying to turn back up the slope, and the men who appeared and disappeared in the dust were kept busy keeping them headed as they wanted them.

Fitch grinned as he reached the split-rail fence where the honeysuckle was already beginning to put on buds. Lying there, he skinned under the bottom rail and scrabbled into the shelter of the side porch. Kate met him at the door and he whipped inside.

"What's all that going on over yonder?" she asked as she helped him beat the dust from himself. "Sounds like a stampede, but there've never been enough cattle in the creek valley to make up a stampede like that. Mostly young stuff ranges down here. We always kept the big bunches driven off so they wouldn't trample the crops."

"I've an idea they've spent all day rounding up enough to make a stampede," George answered. "We hit 'em hard this morning. Took out six or seven men, I estimate. Maybe more. Could be, some of the rest are wounded, too. They looked down-creek for us, burnt John's house where we made it look as if we had camped. Tracks says they may try to hit you in the confusion made by the herd."

"That makes sense," Kate mused. "If they could flush you all out of hiding and get rid of us in the same operation, they'd be ahead of the game. Couldn't be Otis's figuring, though. If his head was as thin as his brain, his hat would fall down around his neck."

"We watched the search party go by. There was a great big fellow with a face the color of a dead fish's belly. Pale eyes. No expression. I felt he was one of those men whom you meet sometimes—terribly smart and without any feelings at all. He gave all of us the collywobbles. You know who I'm talking about?"

"Ah!" Kate breathed. "Sam Garvin. He came about two years ago, after Otis had been making a lot of trouble for us. Your pa said when he first laid eyes on him that he was dangerous. Dangerous and bad clean through. Said he's the kind that could bite a rattlesnake and kill him dead. Robin was killed just after he got here." She cocked her head to look into his eyes.

"We've got the feeling that Garvin is some kind of go-between for Otis and his backers."

"Mark Trant thinks his backers are railroad people. More I think about it, the more sense it makes. Major Haig, back in Arizona, was from a big-money family back East. I heard him talking with Captain Linder, once, about the empires some of his old friends were building, along with their railroads. Where there's enough money behind and enough incentive in front, a lot of mighty bad things get done in the middle. And I think we're right in the middle of that kind of thing right now."

"Well, how and why don't make much difference right at this point," Kate said. "The thing we've got to do is get through the night. They've never hit me at night, it's reasonable to assume that this time they just may. If Garvin is making their plans now, that's the thing we can look for. The unexpected.

"And another thing bothers me a lot Old Syl Graham is 'way down-creek with nobody but Em and that old Digger squaw he picked up somewhere and nursed back to health. Em is a mighty good hand at working or fighting, but the three of them are just as vulnerable as the three of us were, before you came. Even if they are five miles below John's place, Elliot and Garvin might just figure to clean them out, too, in this one sweep. What do you think?"

"I think that nothing will be done against you until the middle of the night. If I can get out onto the range without being spotted, I can cut straight down, not following the creek, and be there in an hour and a half. If they've a spare horse, so Outlaw won't get run to death, we could be back here by midnight. Maybe. If everything goes off just right. You think it's worth risking being hit shorthanded?"

"It's worth it. Syl has been a mighty good neighbor to us, even if he did just about lose his mind when Young Syl disappeared. I'd never rest easy if we let his family get wiped out just to make sure we were a little safer."

Fitch nodded, a short jerk of the chin. "That's Ma," he said to Ab, who had sat quietly while they talked, running his fingers slowly up and down the stock of the rifle in his lap. "You think so, too, Pa?"

Ab nodded wordlessly. Fitch looked at him closely, and he found that the lined face was so weary he wondered how the man held up his head. The effort of forming words was, at the moment, beyond him.

George laid his hand on Ab's shoulder. "You rest some, Pa. There's a long spell of waiting ahead.

You let Ma help you lie down. She'll call you when there's need."

Kate smiled, but her expression was strained. "He hasn't eaten enough to keep a cat alive this past month. And he's not sleeping, I know. I'm worried about him, Son. He was doing so well until Elliot started this last push against us last month. It's set him back almost to the beginning."

Ab reached over to take her work-worn hand. He reached up his left hand and laid it over George's. "All...right," he struggled to say. "Get Elliot! Then...all...fine."

"If I live, Pa, I'll get Elliot. That's a promise. And we're going to send as many of his killers to hell with him as we can. Herb and Pink and Tracks are up the hill right now, just waiting for the chance. As I go by John's place, I'll pick up those bombs, too. We just may need 'em tonight." Without waiting for long goodbyes, he turned and slipped out the side door, after looking and listening acutely for a long moment.

It was easy getting back up the hill, for it was now twilight, and anything more than a few yards away was only a blur of gray. As he neared the thick brush, he whistled his three short notes before rising to walk into the wood. Herb's voice whispered gruffly ahead of him, "All fine here. Come on in."

In a few sentences he told them of his need to go south down-creek and warn or bring back the Grahams. "I think there won't be anything doing for a long time. They must get those crazy cows out of their hair before they can accomplish much. You can't take cover for shooting where a wild-eyed animal is going to run right over you. I think Outlaw and I can make it there and back pretty fast without

102

breaking his wind. You may want to ease down closer around the house so you can get anybody who comes with a torch in a crossfire."

"You go," said Tracks Through the Air. "We take care here. Hurry up, you miss fun."

Fitch grinned into the darkness. "So long," he breathed, and went to locate Outlaw. In ten minutes, he had made it out onto the rangeland, where more secure footing allowed him to let Outlaw into a lope.

He knew these lands as only a man raised in the country can know it. Every fold of the grassland, every silhouetted contour of the rise toward the creek ridge told him surely his position in relation to the valley beyond the ridge. He cut inward toward the John Fitch house, and the smell of smoke greeted him.

Leaving Outlaw just below the ridge, Fitch stole through the overgrown garden spot into the yard, whose fence had already fallen down—or been pulled down. The shape of the squatty smokehouse rose against the stars, and he flitted across the fire-warmed yard to its door.

The thought of Sylvanus Graham hanging there, smiling inscrutably and invisibly at him, wasn't a pleasant one, but Fitch squeezed around the doorway, avoiding the spot as well as he could, and reached high. The lumpy bulk of the bag touched his hand, and he lifted it from its hook.

There was a click of a hoof against pebbles, and he froze as he was, straining his ears through the night. A low mutter of voices rose at some distance, and he inched the smokehouse door shut, closing himself into its acrid darkness with its other tenant.

The voices came closer. Fitch stood silent, his back cricked by his awkward position, dictated by the presence of the body. His mind was working overtime, but the only answer he could come up with was that some of the riders who had gone south were checking on the success of their fire of the late afternoon. He cursed them long and silently.

Shut into the airless space, with the smell of the corpse sickening, Fitch breathed shallowly while he waited. The man who had been his friend hung there within hand's reach. George had no doubt that he had met his end at the hands of one or more of the men who now laughed raucously, if a bit nervously, around the smoldering timbers of the house. Rage joined the sickness in him, and he had to hold himself in check to keep from bursting out among them, Colt blazing.

It seemed an age, but it couldn't have been more than ten minutes or so that they milled around in the yard. Then the thump of hooves in the soil and the clatter against pebbles along the creek announced their departure. Fitch waited another five minutes to make certain all of them were gone; then he moved out of the smokehouse, carefully handling his bomb bag.

Outlaw had waited, quiet and patient, in the spot where George had left him. In two minutes, they were again out in the open country, heading south. They went fast, as the short rest had given the horse new wind. Though George still felt his reasoning to be sound, something about the feel of the night filled him with apprehension. He was driven to hurry and he gave in to the compulsion.

They eased over the high ground toward the Graham house well within the time limits Fitch had set for himself. There was no light showing through the chinks around the shutters. Nothing seemed to move in the blackness of the barn lot or yard, yet Fitch pulled in and dismounted, tethering Outlaw to a tree in the orchard. Then he cat-footed toward the house, every sense honed to keenness. Something was badly amiss. All his well developed instincts told him as much.

The house loomed before him, a low bulk of darkness against the stars. He slid up against the wall beside the bedroom window and set his ear against the wood. He thought he could detect a faint sound. Raising his head, he checked for breeze moving branches against the shingles or the walls, but there was no wind at all. The night was as still as death.

Again he listened, focusing all his attention through his ears. There was a rasp of breath in the room beyond the wall. Not the breathing of a well and uninjured person, but a painful indrawing of air, followed at a long interval by an equally painful expulsion. There was no other sound at all. Not even the gnawing of a rat or the call of a night bird.

Finally, reassured, he rapped his nails lightly against the window and whispered, "Mr. Graham? Em? Who's in there?"

The rasp of breath stopped for a moment. Then Sylvanus Graham's well-remembered voice said, "I'm here. Who is that, out there? If you're Elliot's man, you know damn well what was done here this evenin'. If you're not, come in here and untie me. I'm about done in."

"It's George Fitch," whispered George. "I came down here to warn you they might hit you tonight, but looks like I'm too late. Where's your daughter and Lill?"

As he spoke, he came around by the porch and entered the room, keeping low so his shape wouldn't show against the sky in the doorway. "Where are you?" he called.

"Over to your left, in the corner by the window. There ought to be a lamp on the table just to the right of the door. Hurry!"

Fitch felt to his right, and his fingers gingerly touched the glass globe of an oil lamp. In a second, he had a match to its wick and could see around the room. It was undamaged, orderly as it had always been.

"They must have surprised you," he said as he cut the thongs that held the old man's wrists to pegs, which had been driven into the wall above his head. Then he got a good look at Graham and swallowed hard. "My God!" he choked. "What happened here, Mr. Syl?"

Graham fell forward into his arms, and he carried him over to the bed and laid him on the clean but faded quilt. Evidently, the raiders had strung him up and then shot him up. There were bloody holes in both shoulders, several in each arm, one in his right leg. His right ear was half shot away. Blood covered him, but it had begun to dry, stiffening his clothing.

George was aghast. He had so little time before he would be needed back at his mother's house, and Graham needed so much attention. The task was, he felt certain, far beyond his skill, for blood loss had turned the man's skin bluish. He was only half conscious, and George felt that only a terrible act of will had allowed him to answer the call at the window. Shock and chill would kill him before the night was out, if something wasn't done.

Graham's eyelids flickered, and George bent over him, tucking blankets about his shoulders. "Mr. Syl! Mr. Syl! What happened to Em? Where's old Lill? Are they hurt, too? I need to look for them, if they're here."

The answering voice was a groan. "Lill's shut in woodshed," he gasped. "She hid in there, and they just propped the door shut with a log and left her to starve. Em...George, they took Em!"

"Took her!" Fitch tried for a moment to think why anyone would want to kidnap the hard-headed sixteen-year-old that he had known. Then he realized that she would now be a woman of twenty-eight. He couldn't imagine her being beautiful, but nothing was impossible.

Graham interrupted his wondering. "Elliot came courtin' her when he first came to the valley. Em's a determined woman. You may remember how she was from a kid. She'd turned down better men than Elliot. She likes the place here, likes handlin' the crops and cattle. Good as any man I ever knew at ranch work. She'd no idea of marryin', and particularly not marryin' Otis Elliot. She said she could wring him out and hang him up to dry if she wanted to. She hates a weaklin'."

George was now kneeling before the fireplace that had been built to face two ways, into the bedroom and also into the kitchen, using the same stack for two different hearths. As the kindling caught, and the room warmed, the old man's color grew a bit better. He closed his eyes again, and George touched his forehead after he had the fire going well.

"I'm going after Lill. Be right back. You lie still, now, Mr. Syl. We'll take care of things. We'll get Em back, too." He went quietly out onto the porch and looked about to locate the woodshed.

It had been moved since he had been on the Graham place. It was joined onto the creek side of the back porch, and he could see, in the faint glimmer of star shine, a heavy log leaned against the low doorway. He had it away in an instant, and then he eased the door open.

"Lill! It's George Fitch. I've got Mr. Syl in the bedroom, and he's hurt pretty bad. Come quick!"

There was a rustle of motion in the dark interior of the shed. Then a hand reached out and caught at his elbow, and he helped the old woman to crawl out of her cramped prison. She was even thinner than he remembered as he put his arm about her shoulders and half carried her into the house.

There, under her direction, he found the kettle and set it on the hearth, rummaged clean cotton from a cabinet for making bandages, and brewed some pungent herb tea, which she drank thirstily. With that in her system, she seemed to regain vigor, and her first act was to urge another cup down Syl Graham.

The hot liquid seemed to give him new strength, and he talked feverishly, as the two warmed blankets to cover him with, then checked each of the wounds for bad bleeding. Only two were bleeding freely, the others having clotted enough to await later treatment.

"You'd never know Em, now," the old man babbled, as George gently probed the wound in his right shoulder from which blood still was oozing steadily. "She made a fine-lookin' woman. Grew a

108

lot after you left, George. She's tall and slim, now. All that red hair turned darker, and she lost her freckles 'long about the time she was twenty-two. She had traders and cowpokes and all kinds of young men makin' trails across the countryside for years, but she never saw a one she cottoned to. Trouble was, she's a better man than most men, and she wasn't about to tie up with somebody she looked down on.

"Come to lookin' down—Otis Elliot was the one she mighty nigh had to bend over to even see! Never could abide that slab-sided egg-sucker. He came ridin' up here a few months after he moved in up-creek and gave her to know he was givin' her the honor of his attention. That gal could always skin a fence post with her tongue, and she let him have it head-on. All those ten-dollar words she learns out of the books she sends East for just about swamped him. His hands were sittin' around on the porch listenin', and that just about finished him off, 'cause they began snickerin'.

"So you can see why Elliot felt like he had a grudge against her and me. Goddamn, George! What you doin'?" the man interjected as George extracted the slug and poured in a dollop of whiskey.

"Lie still, now, Mr. Syl," he said, looking over to see that Lill had cleaned the other bad wound. "We'll finish getting the lead out of you tomorrow. Right now I've got to leave you with Lill because I think that crew is going to hit my folks' place in another hour. I've got to run the hooves off Outlaw to get there. Can you make it?"

Syl Graham grunted. "Bullet ain't been cast that can kill me," he said. "Pour some of that likker in the right spot, and I'll come with you."

109

Fitch laughed. "I'll come back for you later. You and Lill can stay with us until we can figure out a way to get Em back. See you, Mr. Syl."

The old man grunted in reply as Lill poured more liquor into a wound, and George eased the door open and slipped out into the night. Looking at the house, he was happy to see that no light showed on the side nearest the creek, and little was visible around the shutters he had closed across the bedroom window. The smell of wood smoke was unmistakable, but he felt that enough had worked its way down the creek valley on the night winds so that anyone investigating for Elliot might well think it came from the burned John Fitch house.

Fitch hurried upslope to the spot where Outlaw waited. He was relieved to find the horse well rested after the fast journey he had made. Slipping the bit back behind the horse's teeth, he led it over the scrub-covered ridge onto the clear ground.

He looked up at the stars. Damn! It would have to be a fast trip to get him home in time. He had a feeling in his bones that he might arrive too late after all his efforts. But he mounted and touched his un-spurred heel to Outlaw's flank. The gelding took off northward, and the *ta-ta-ta-thump* of his hooves drowned out the lonely calls of the coyotes and the night birds as George Fitch headed for home.

CHAPTER EIGHT

It was past midnight, but not much, when Fitch reined in his mount and walked him cautiously up under the rise of the ridge. He tethered the horse well inside the stand of trees above his parents' house; then he gave a sleepy twitter of a whistle, just enough to alert his companions to his presence. From ahead and to his right came a matching twitter, and he found himself looking at a bulk that could only be that of Herb Yardley as it detached itself from the tree shadow and loomed before him.

"Two riders come down-creek about a quarter hour ago, George," the big man whispered. "Passed by as if they wuz goin' on down, then crossed the creek just below the bend and sneaked back through the trees on this side. Pink's up above 'em, right under that big cottonwood. Tracks slipped down to the house and said he'd watch from the barn loft. Said he can't run like he used to, so he'd better be there close to begin with. He thinks they're goin' to try to finish this place up tonight. Damn Injun! He kin see things I'd jist as soon not know about."

"What do you think Herb?" Fitch asked as he hunkered down into the shadows and scrutinized the faint glimmer that marked the creek.

"I think the old bastard's right as rain," Herb growled. "I think they've been doin' their worst down-creek, too. You smell like smoke an' dead meat. They burnt the Grahams out, too?"

"No, but they hit 'em. Almost killed the old man —strung him up on his own wall and used him for target practice. Took the girl with 'em. She'd turned Otis down, the old fellow told me. I stink from hiding in that damn smokehouse with young Syl, while those coyotes sniffed around the house to make sure it was burned to the ground. I've got the bag of bombs right back there in the bushes behind me."

"Well, that shoots my plan," Herb grunted. "I'd thought we might leave a couple here to keep the raiders busy an' go back up an' blow Otis's house to Kingdom Come. Can't do that if he's got the Graham girl there. Damn! I think it would've worked."

Fitch turned his head toward that dark shape in surprise. "You know, I think it would've worked, too. I couldn't see it for worrying about my kin, but it would have been the one thing Elliot wouldn't expect. Too bad."

From up-creek came a faint sound, almost unidentifiable in the clutter of night sounds. Fitch cocked his head, and memories came flooding back.

"Ssss!" he hissed. "Bunch of 'em are coming. Got their horses' hooves muffled so they won't make any noise. We'd better get those bombs and snake on down there. I think they're going to try to slip up on the house instead of making a frontal attack. I'd do it that way, myself, if I were Garvin."

Carefully, he moved backward until he touched the bag with its lumpy cargo. Then he followed Herb down the slope, tacking back and forth to take advantage of every clump of scrub, every rock.

Even as dark as the night was, they knew their shapes could show up black against the paler stuff of the soil that slanted upward behind them.

They stopped at the yard fence. There, George divided up the remaining bombs and found to his satisfaction that a good dozen and a half were still in the sack. He tore the tough cloth into two parts, and Herb gathered his share into it and crept away to the right, toward the barn where Tracks was waiting. George gave him time to reach the shelter, then he holstered his handgun again and moved off to the left.

It was awkward going, keeping his own profile below the top fence rail and also moving the bag silently. Snagged for the tenth time by a trailing runner of rose vine, he was patiently unsnarling it from his own sleeve when a sound froze him to stillness. He turned his head very slowly, surveying every inch of terrain that he could see.

Three good-sized trees were clumped together some ten yards to his left and slightly upslope, though here the slope eased to the flat bench on which Ab had built his house. Something had scrubbed against the rough bark there. The sound had been so slight that if George had been moving, himself, he might well have missed it. But now that he knew where to look, he realized that the bases of two of the trees were thicker than they should have been. Men crouched behind them, and in the faint light from the stars, Fitch could see the glint of the Colts in their hands.

As he sank silently into the thorny concealment of the rose vines, he could hear the riders on the other side of the house as they approached the darkened structure. A horse's gut rumbled. Another whiffled through his nostrils. He felt that he could hear even the breathing of the men who rode them, so keenly was his hearing honed.

Turning his back to hide the glow, he lit a cigar that he had kept in his pocket for just such use. He touched its red tip to the wick of a bomb, whirled in his tracks, ignoring the clutch of the vines, and hurled it between the trees.

There was a *wump* of sound, as he fell flat and heard a hail of shrapnel go zinging over, shredding vines and thunking into the fence rails. Strangled gasps and moans from the trees were answered by a yell from the creek as the attackers came in fast, abandoning their attempt at secrecy. Fitch rose without another glance at the place where the two had been and made for the corner of the fencerow.

Behind him, he heard a chuckle. "Nice piece of work, I do say," Pincus Wills remarked as he came up to the fence. "Now you go off where you've a mind to, an' I'll cover you from here. I kin get anybody that tries to come around to flank us. Take a batch of them bombs, too. Handiest little do-gadgets I've seen in a long time. Mind the Minié balls in the war? Puts me in mind of them little devils."

Fitch eased his way along the fence as a crackle of shots sounded from the house. He heard the scream of a wounded horse; then a patter of slugs hit the solid log walls. Now he was around the corner, coming down the shadow line of the fence toward the main bunch of the raiders. The glow of his cigar betrayed him, and he dropped to avoid the swarm of bullets that came at him from the massed group that was slowed by his father's solid rail fence. Again he touched his cigar to a fuse, took the bomb in his left hand, and slung it at the dark blot of men and horses.

The bomb hit among them, and there was a mad scramble to get out of its way before it exploded. As the men milled, the big shotgun roared from the house, and its noise was echoed by the bomb under their feet. Those who were left able to run took off, some afoot, leaving wounded horses to their fates. The flat between the house and the creek was clear.

George vaulted over the fence and whistled as he hit the porch. The door opened and he slid inside where his mother's tense face awaited him. "They gone, George?"

"For a little, anyway. If I read Garvin, he won't let a setback stop him for long. I'd bet money he has more men waiting up-creek, ready to hit us when we think we're safe."

"So you're going to go after 'em before they can get down here," she finished for him, and he grinned at her in the faint light from the coals on the hearth.

"I'll leave Tracks in the barn loft. He can't move all that fast, but with a bunch of bombs to hand, he can make himself felt. Herb and Pink will go with me, and we'll see if we can't make it lively for anybody who gets here too late for the dance."

Ab's painful croak came from the chair beside the window. "Old Syl? He...all...right?"

"Hurt bad. Lill's taking care of him, and I think he'll do. But they took Em with them."

He heard his mother's breath pass her throat in a whistle. Looking down, he saw an expression that he had never seen on her face before.

"George," she said, her eyes fierce in the fire-light, "so help me, I'll hang that bastard myself. It's on my account he came here. If I hadn't been kin, he'd never have known about Sweetwater Creek.

"Em's been my anchor and my strength through all this. She stood up to Elliot and all his men until they backed down. She's come all the way up here to check on us, even when it wasn't safe for her to get outside her own porch. Otis Elliot isn't fit to dig out her privy. Get him, George. Bring him alive if you can."

Fitch put his arm about her shoulders and kissed her cheek. "If I can, I will," he promised. "Now I've got to go. Garvin will be bringing more men against us, I'm certain. We've got to get in position before they come. God bless!"

He went out the back bedroom window, and Tildy barred the shutters behind him. A whistle toward the barn and the fence brought Herb and Pink ghosting to his side.

Standing below the barn loft door so that Tracks could hear, he told them what he suspected.

"Sounds reasonable," Pink drawled. "We kin get our evenin's exercise. Good for the health. You notice old Herb here ain't even sneezed since we went after them Apach' horses? Nothin' like action to clean out the system."

Tracks grunted. His voice was barely audible, nearby though they were, as he said, "Watch big man. Tricky. Watch all sides. Men in bunch, they not all. Keep eye behind you."

Fitch nodded, though he knew the old Indian couldn't see him. "Will do, Tracks Through the Air. And thanks. If anything happens...we're square and then some. Take care!"

Without speaking, the three whites slipped through the rails of the lot fence and moved out

116

through the scrub that flanked the enclosure. Taking advantage of every bit of cover, they sped up-creek, angling inward toward the point George had chosen for their ambush. Now they weren't burdened with the bombs, for all had been left behind with Tracks in the loft. They well knew that any glowing cigar end would bring a hail of instant death from those enemies who had learned the lesson twice.

George had traded Tildy his rifle for her big shotgun. In these before-dawn hours, accuracy was a thing not to be expected, and a rifle was merely a hindrance. Herb and Pink had left their long guns behind also, being armed with handguns only. For close work, which they intended that this would be, those would do best.

Pink dropped out of their line beside the creek and disappeared beneath the low lip of the bank at a spot where the trail skirted it closely in an area without trees. Fifty yards further on, Herb melted his bulk into a patch of scrub. Looking back, Fitch couldn't see so much as a leaf quiver to betray his presence. George himself went to a sandy spot well short of the arm of woods that had been the site of their first ambush. There he wriggled himself into the soil itself, using a scanty tangle of brush to hide the presence of his weapon, which he placed carefully, ready-aimed at the point where the trail left the trees.

Mindful of Tracks's parting advice, he placed himself so that his vision could sweep a good one hundred and eighty-degree field, without turning his head. Then he waited, knowing that if his guess had been correct, the wait would not be long.

It wasn't. He could feel the vibration of hooves that moved slowly along the trail a long time before the first horse came through the trees. They came cautiously, and he knew that Tracks had been correct. Outriders protected the flanks of the group that showed only as a dark bulk in the night.

With his inborn instinct for tactics, Fitch had placed himself and his few men right in the middle of their enemies, who were watching everywhere but there. He waited until the lead horse was almost upon him before crooking his finger around the trigger of the shotgun. As its sonorous boom scattered dismay among the riders, he rolled clear of the spot where he had been, taking the gun along with him. Another blast caught the dancing horses and the cursing men from the other side.

Now he could hear the pounding hooves of the mounts of the outriders as they hurried to help their companions. He melted back, invisible against the earth, letting his enemies shoot blindly at each other and their approaching fellows. Finding the creek, he stepped into its pebbled edge and moved down toward Pink, letting the ripple of the water cover any sound his booted feet might make.

As he neared the spot where Wills waited, he hissed softly between his teeth. A hand rose from invisibility and pulled him down beside the skinny little man.

"Sounds like you got 'em stirred up pretty good," he breathed in Fitch's ear. "All that shootin' they're doin' jest makes our job easier."

"They're not sure how many there are of us," Fitch murmured. "I hit 'em from two sides with the shotgun, and then they got to banging away until nobody could have said how many had attacked 'em. They'll sort it out in a minute. I'd guess Garvin was back behind with another batch, and he'll

118

straighten 'em up in a hurry. I'll go give Herb a hand. You all right here?"

"Jest fine," said Pincus. "A mite chilly in this spring air, but a man can't have everything. You make that Herb keep his big head down. Man that size makes a hell of a target!"

There was real concern in the small man's voice, and Fitch grinned as he moved up beside the trail and sank into a clump of scrub that matched Herb's, a bit farther on. Once settled, he twittered his signal call, knowing that the huge trapper would hear it, even through the racket of gunshots, horse squeals, and shouts.

A big voice was booming out now, and Fitch felt sure that it was Garvin's. The voice matched the man, huge and overbearing, yet strangely toneless. A monotony of indistinguishable words poured out, up there in the darkness, and the three in concealment waited patiently. But something in the way the approaching riders moved alerted Fitch to a change when they finally got themselves organized. In a flash, he understood that Garvin had spread them thinly across the west side of the valley so that nobody could catch them bunched again.

He hissed viciously, and in a moment he felt Herb's presence beside him. He touched his arm and pulled the big man back toward the creek bank where Pink was concealed. Once they were well under that protective overhang, he drew their heads close to his own.

"We've got to hit 'em fast with one good sweep. Then we make tracks across the creek and through the brush, clear up across the ridge on the other side. Without making any noise, boys. There're too many of them and too few of us to stand up to a toe-to-toe

119

battle right now. There must be a good dozen coming at us right now. Ready?"

He felt rather than saw their two nods; then the three rose to their knees, their eyes just above the level of the bank, and saw the first riders silhouetted against the stars.

CHAPTER NINE

Their eyes, now long used to the night, could pick out the shapes as darker patches moving strung out along and on either side of the trail. Fitch waited until the first ones had passed; then he touched Herb and Pink, in turn. They leveled their weapons and opened fire, blazing away as fast as the handguns would work and he could reload the shotgun. Gaps appeared in the dark line.

The night filled, once again, with screams and yells and the awful cries of horses. Garvin's voice rose in wrathful coldness, and Fitch drew his companions back under the creek bank as a storm of lead swept up and down, blindly seeking the source of the ambush. When it stopped, he led the way up-creek in the shelter of the bank, then across a sandy patch of shallows and into heavy scrub that lined its other side.

Behind them, they heard the remainder of Garvin's crew pulling themselves together, calling out to find who was dead or wounded. Crashing told them that Garvin had sent horsemen down into the creek, suspecting that it had sheltered the bushwhackers. But they were well away, almost to the ridge by now, hidden among the generous belt of trees that accompanied the Sweetwater all the way along its journey to join the Canadian River.

Once over the ridge, they ran like demons, stumbling in their heeled boots but making good time, nevertheless. Now the sky was growing lighter, too, which aided their flight. The three miles that separated the place of ambush from the Fitch place they cut to less than two by going straight, instead of following the windings of the creek. So they came with the sunrise down the slope toward the house where Kate waited.

Staggering down the last of the way, Fitch felt as if his legs were about to play out on him. He had ridden and run and waited and watched for one of the longest days he could remember. The previous night's sleep was almost forgotten, and his eyes felt as if they had been poked back into his *skull* with sticks. His whistle of warning to his mother was lacking in its usual crispness.

Herb looked around at him, his eyebrows raised. Fitch grinned grayly. "Mighty near too tired to pucker," he said.

They went directly to the house. If Garvin's men still had the vinegar to be watching and waiting to hit them, then so be it. The three were just too weary to worry about it. The brief rest they had had wasn't enough to keep them going indefinitely.

Kate whipped the door open and shut in one continuous motion. Her shrewd eyes sized them up before George had time to say a word, and she gestured toward the kitchen. "Tildy and I figured you'd be worn out and starving...if you got back at all. Eat some breakfast, then go in and sleep. I went out early, before light, and moved your horses into the barn with ours, shut in out of sight with plenty of hay. You've got to rest. We can handle things by daylight. Garvin isn't fond of coming right up so you can see him when he does his shenanigans.

"Tracks is watching in the barn. He sleeps like a cat. You can wrinkle a leaf a mile away and he snaps awake, so he got a good night's sleep. We dozed off and on, knowing that you were between them and us. We're in good shape, even your pa."

George sighed and let the shotgun slip into its accustomed corner of the room. "I'm not as young as I was," he mourned, sitting down to ease the boots from his battered feet. "Ten years back, I could run all day, fight all night, and go to a dance the next day. Thirty isn't twenty, Ma."

Kate grinned. "Don't tell me, George. I found that out twenty years ago. Now you go in with Pink and Herb and wash up. If Sam Garvin comes calling, I'll wake you up. Otherwise, I don't want to hear a peep out of you until about sundown. We need you three bright-eyed and bushy-tailed, when the time comes."

Evidently Garvin didn't have any taste for calling on the Fitches that day, for George fell into deep slumber at once, with his belly full of ham and pancakes, and slept so deeply that no dream troubled him. He woke in one swoop, as he had for nearly a dozen years, remembering his location, the situation, and assessing the time and conditions in an automatic sequence. The mellow sunlight streaking the far wall told him that he had, as directed, slept the day all but through. He looked at the bunk opposite his own and saw that Herb and Pink had awakened before him. Their boots and gun belts were gone from the wall hooks and shelf that had been put up for the use of the Fitch sons so many years before.

Groaning, he sat up and swung his legs over the side of the bed. Something had come to him, either in the midst of sleep or at the point of waking. He pulled on his boots, fastened his belt, and went up the hall to the kitchen, where the smell of fresh coffee met him.

"Whooh! I can use a cup of that," he told Kate as she turned to greet him. "All the time I've been gone from home, I've thought of your coffee. How you can take the same stuff I boil up and make it taste like you do, I'll never figure out."

"Sit down and eat," she said, setting a steaming cup before him. "Then tell me what it is you've got in your head now. I know that look in your eye. But eat first!"

When he had packed away enough to satisfy her, George leaned his elbows on the table and looked first at Kate, then at Ab, who had been helped into the kitchen while Tildy stood watch. "I've got to go see Eck Margrave," he said.

Ab frowned, and Kate, reading him with the accuracy of long marriage, said, "It's a good way down to the settlement, George. And Eck's been ordered to keep out of this. The railroad, if that's who it is, doesn't want anybody poking into this mess until everything's under control. The marshal's office was polite as could be, and I could see Eck was itching to take a hand, but he told me straight out that he'd be out fast if he did."

"Still, he doesn't know I'm back, much less with help. It's kind of like the army. If you don't go by the book and fail, it's your neck, but if you succeed, you're a hero. We've killed a few of Elliot's hands

124

and messed up a lot more. He's going to be going into town to find replacements. If Eck could just put a spoke in that, it'd help. And if he thinks the big-wigs just might lose out on this particular little deal, he might go out on a limb. He's a stuffed shirt, but he was always honest."

"So off you go, wearing some poor horse's hooves off, not to mention the seat of your own britches. I swear, George, if you weren't right so of-ten, I'd get purely outdone with you. But I see what you're thinking. If we happen to win up here, we'll need somebody to speak out for us if the backers decide to make trouble for us."

"I hate to leave you, but if I'm going to, I think now is the time. It will take Garvin a while to get his troops organized again. He may even have to go for replacements before he feels confident he can take us. And now that Elliot's gone and kidnapped Emily Graham, I think even a tame marshal may take an interest. Nobody's going to take kindly to messing around with women, and I think they've over-stepped themselves on this one."

"Well, if you're going, it's about time. The sun's down, and nobody's been in sight all day. Tracks swears there aren't even any watchers in the trees or on the ridge. You'd better take Sunspur. He hasn't been worked for awhile, and he's full of vinegar. He's not as fast as Outlaw, but he's a goer, and Outlaw likely needs a good rest after yesterday. From what Tracks tells me, that horse is something special." Kate smiled at her son, but the shadow of worry was on her face as she watched him.

George rolled his head on his shoulders, work-ing loose the knot of tension that still held him, de-spite his long rest. All those years of refusing to be rushed, of making time wait on him, now seemed to be falling in on him at once. He needed, at that moment, to be in three places: on his way to see the marshal, hidden in the trees to watch for any movement on the part of Elliot's henchmen, and down at Syl Graham's. He shrugged on his jacket, reached down his battered hat from the old peg where it had always hung when he was at home, and turned to his mother.

"Be back just as quick as I can, Ma. If nothing seems likely to happen, you might see if Herb or Pink would be willing to check on old Syl. He was plumb full of lead, and Lill has her hands full, I know."

Kate nodded. "Somebody'll get down there. I may go myself. I'll be more help than anybody. God knows, I've had plenty of recent practice at treating gunshot wounds."

George opened his mouth to protest. Then he closed it again. His mother was, he well knew, able to care for herself and anybody else at hand. Only the terrible odds she had faced had made her send for him. She would pay no more attention to cautions and worryings than he would, himself. He grinned at her, feeling the warm surge of confidence inside that went back to his boyhood relationship with both his parents.

Without another word, he went to the back window and opened the shutter a crack. He could see nothing out of the ordinary through the thickening twilight. In one slick motion, he was out and skitting for the yard fence. He followed its shelter around to the barn lot where he whistled for Tracks. The old Indian twittered a reply, and George went into the barn. He spoke to Outlaw, stroking his nose for a moment, then left the gelding to his hay. Beyond him, the horses they had stolen from the Apache munched quietly. His mother's mare, Valley, was beyond them, flanked by her colt and the stallion, Sunspur, who snorted at the unfamiliar hand that bridled him.

"You go to settlement," Tracks said, and it wasn't a question. Fitch was getting used to the old Indian's ability to read things out of thin air, so he nodded.

"Maybe get law to help. Likely not, mebbeso. Man there, though. Find. Little short man, skinny like Pink. Black suit, white shirt, shiny hat. He help."

"A gunfighter?" asked Fitch, interested in spite of himself.

"Not gunfighter. Not know what. Just find. He help."

George tightened the cinch and led Sunspur out into the thickening darkness. "I'll do my best, Tracks. You've known what you were talking about so far. I'll bank on this time, too. Take care of 'em all while I'm gone."

The only reply was a grunt from the shadows inside the barn, and he turned the stallion's head toward the settlement and stole out of the creek valley onto the high grassland. He had ridden this country for half his life. Not a mile of it had missed his repeated passings as he looked for strayed cattle and lost calves. The contours of the horizon against the sky told him exactly where he was as he galloped, walked, galloped, walked, then rested the horse.

The patch of stars that he was using as a guide had moved some quarter way across the heavens by the time the lights of Solano were sparsely scattered before him. George was a bit surprised to find any lights still showing at all, for the tiny settlement usually went to bed with the sun. He figured quickly, for he had lost track of the days since he had begun his journey.

"Saturday night," he grunted to himself. "Must be more ranch hands around than there used to be. Wouldn't have been worth keeping the saloon open for, otherwise."

There were a few riders in the street as he rode in. Most of them seemed to be heading home for the night, which told him that the Golden Finger Saloon hadn't improved its entertainment much since his own salad days. It did help to make him less conspicuous as he hitched his horse in a scant row of others and ambled down the street toward the marshal's office where one dim lamp burned behind the dusty window.

As quiet as the town seemed, George hadn't any notion that Eck would be on duty so late. Only the tinkle of a badly played piano made any dent at all in the stillness, and his own footsteps sounded a bit too loud as he entered the office and took off his hat.

The deputy marshal was a youngster he had never seen before. He looked up as Fitch passed the doorway, his eyes indifferent. "Do fer you?" he mumbled.

"Just like to know if the marshal's in town, now. I need to see him about some business, and I didn't want to go all the way out to his house and wake up his family to no purpose," George said.

"He's s'posed to be home. Come by here about six o'clock to check things out, then headed that way. You one of them Easterners he's been talkin' to?"

Fitch looked at the deputy in wonder. If he could mistake a hard-bitten cavalry veteran for an eastern dude, he was one of the really classic cases of stupidity in all history. But he only smiled and said, "Thank you. I think I'll ride out and see him tonight. I've got to travel tomorrow. He still sit up and read till all hours?"

"Damn sure does! Durndest thing I ever knowed, a full-growed man sittin' around readin' books!"

"Then I'll bid you good night." Fitch looked up and down the street before he made his way back to the spot where his stallion was hitched. Sunspur was dancing with disgust at being hitched. His life had been spent either being ridden, grazing free, or unhindered in a spacious barn with hay to make the confinement palatable. He didn't like this new thing at all.

As Fitch pulled loose the reins, a man who had been leaning in the shadow of the porch in front of the general store stood straight, then stepped forward.

"Real nice horse you have there, sir," he said, and Fitch identified his eastern twang before he got a good look at the man himself.

Then he could see him by the light of the lamp shining inside the saloon next door. Black suit. White shirt. Beaver hat with a shiny band around the crown. It could only be the man Tracks had urged him to find.

"He's a pretty good mount," George answered, slapping the reins against his palm. "Not used to my kind of working, but he's got bottom to him."

The other man eased over toward the lighted window until George, too, was in its light. "I'm Arthur Hastings," he said. "Been here for two weeks in that mouse hole of a hotel, and not one thing has happened worth writing home about. But when you came riding up the street there, I thought to myself, Arthur, there comes a story, if you ever saw one. That man has serious business here. He carries himself like a man who's used to being shot at, and he rides like cavalry. Now what could he be wanting in this dusty little hole in the middle of the night?"

Fitch looked him over carefully. The pinched face was unlike the open brown countenances he was used to, but the squinty blue eyes were honest and met his squarely. There was, somehow, a feeling of power about the scrawny little man, and Fitch knew the answer before he phrased his next question. "You talk like a newspaper reporter. Are you?"

"Freelance. My stuff is carried in everything from the New York papers to the dime novels. You look like somebody who needs a handy ear to talk into."

"I just might at that. I'm about to go out to see the marshal at his home. If he decides to help, I may not need a reporter. If he doesn't, I will. Where can I find you? At the hotel?"

"God, no! I moved out of there two days ago. I found a Mrs. Maloney who rents a room the size of an army cot, but she sets a table fit for the gods. I'll be there if you need me. Everybody in the family goes to bed early, but my window is on the south side, next to the vegetable garden. Tap on it, and I'll be right with you. But for heaven's sake, don't step in the squash vines. She fries those things up in a batter, and the chef at Delmonico's would cry with envy to taste them."

Fitch nodded, stepped out of the light, and mounted Sunspur. "See you," he said, and turned the stallion's head southward, toward Eck Margrave's Bar M.

There was one lone light burning in a front window of the big house when Fitch rode up to the veranda. Eck, then, was still in his library, indulging in the habit that had forced him to kill more than one man who contended that one who was a bookworm must also be soft.

He walked quietly across the veranda and tapped on the glass of the study window. The lamp was immediately extinguished, and he heard Eck move across the room to stand flattened by the window.

"Who's there?" he whispered. "Step out in the middle of the porch and drop your weapons. Then I'll see if you ride away or go across a horse."

"It's George Fitch," Fitch said in a quiet voice. "I've come home with some friends to help my folks. I need to talk to you, Eck."

"Ummm. Yes. Come to the front door, George, and I'll let you in. Tie your mount around at the side so nobody who comes sniffing around can see it. We've all got problems, these days."

When they were in the study, the lamp relit and the blinds drawn, George looked closely at the marshal. He was heavier now than he had been twelve years ago, and his curly brown hair was well tracked with gray. His pale eyes, which had always seemed to George more of a scholar's than those of a lawman, had sunk into a mesh of wrinkles until only a glint showed where they were.

"My lord, boy, you've grown up and then some!" the marshal said. "We heard great things of you in the war, even if you were on the wrong side. Now I see you, I understand a lot of things. You've been doing some rough jobs, I'd guess, from the look of you."

"Not as rough as the one I have coming up," George said. "You know what's going on over on the Sweetwater. I understand that there isn't much you're allowed to do, given the political situation. But I need to know if there's anything at all you *can* do."

"I hate it like hell, but there's not. I'm hedged in all around by big-money Easterners, railroad men, and speculators who've got congressmen in every pocket. If I so much as sneeze in the wrong direction, I'm out, and somebody who won't even try to keep the cheap crooks out will take over. I don't like it, but I'm hanging on, trying to figure out what I can do to straighten things out. I've just about given up. They're smart, these men who're trying to take over all the land around. They stay just barely inside the law, or else they hide it mighty well."

"They've kidnapped Emily Graham. Shot her dad full of holes, but he's still alive and may make it. They hit them two days ago, and if I hadn't gone down to check on them, old Syl would have died. Lill, too, because they had locked her in the woodshed. Does that make any difference?"

"It could. It very well might. But I'll have to check it out very carefully, and it'll be a couple of days, anyway, before I could move. I've got to send telegrams, get replies. Takes time."

"Then tell me this, marshal. If we manage to clean out the whole entire rat's nest from Sweetwater, and don't all get killed doing it, will you be duty bound to arrest us? I've got to make my plans on the basis of what you tell me, here and now. They're about to hit us hard, finish us off, tomorrow or the next day. They likely sent into town for some more men yesterday or will tomorrow. Sam Garvin probably's the one who'll come after 'em."

Eck looked sick. "Garvin was in town this afternoon. Picked up a dozen or so hands that I could see. There weren't any real hard cases in town, but they were all young and tough-looking.

"Listen, George. I know you don't really understand why I can't help you. If I wasn't standing in my own shoes, right now, I wouldn't either. But I wish you well. Anything I can do, I will do. And I won't pay any more mind to what you and your friends do to Elliot's bunch than I've been allowed to pay to what they've done to your folks. It's not much, but I promise that. And if pressure comes at me to throw you to the wolves, I'll resign. About Emily Graham—I may be able to get some leverage with that. We don't take kindly to messing with women folks around here."

Fitch took the glass of brandy the big man handed him and tossed it down. It burned all the way down, then kindled a steady glow somewhere around his belt buckle. Then he looked Margrave straight in the eye. "I've always thought a lot of you, Eck. My pa, too. We figure you're doing the best you can, in the circumstances. Just try to do whatever you can manage. That's all we ask.

"There's a newspaper man in town. I'm going to talk to him tonight. Maybe we can bust something loose if we hit them back home where they live."

The marshal lifted his own glass. "It takes awhile, George, to get things written up and in print. But if that Hastings fellow can make a big bang, tell him to go to it. Just try not to make the old man look too bad, eh?"

"Done!" Fitch said. "Now douse that light so I can leave without a crack of light to show where I am. I don't think I was followed, but you never know for sure."

But the night was still, and no hint of any watcher or follower interrupted his ride back to Solano.

CHAPTER TEN

The town was dark when he got back. Only the occasional lantern that some storekeepers hung on the porches of their businesses made puddles of yellow light along the dust of the street. Fitch turned aside into an alley and tied Sunspur to a rail fence that bounded its rear. Then he made his silent way to Mrs. Maloney's, where he had been a few times before. Her daughter, Cathleen, had cut a swath among all the young men when he had been eighteen.

He stepped lightly among the vegetable rows, found Hastings's window, and tapped a pebble against it. For a little while there was no sound inside, and he tapped again.

"Just a minute," came a gruff mumble from the room. "Can't get my damned pants on. Here!"

The window opened, and George went over the sill into Hastings's chamber. It was, literally, not much bigger than the cot he slept on. They were obliged to sit facing each other on it, for there was no room for any other furniture in the place. The candle that Hastings lit showed his belongings hung from the walls, draped over a hook on the inside of the door, and edges of them stuck out from under the bed.

Hastings rummaged under his end of the bed and pulled out a bottle. "Have a drink," he offered. "You look as if things didn't go to suit you."

"Could have been better; could have been worse," George answered. "The marshal has his hands tied. You probably know more about that than I do. They say it's happening all along the proposed rail route. But he won't butt in to stop us, either. He's not happy about things. Not at all."

"I likely know more than you think about your problem," the newsman said, handing him the bottle. "The stories start out much the same. Somebody starts trying to buy up land, then begins to make it rough if people don't sell. Then they start shooting the holdouts, and things go from bad to worse until everyone clears out and leaves an open field to the grabbers. I've tried for six months to find a bunch that's standing fast. I want a story, and that's the only one I'll settle for.

"I used to work for the *Sun* in New York. I got to nosing around in the Washington dealings of the men who own the railroads. They own more than railroads, let me tell you. I got booted out of my job so fast I didn't have time to clear out my desk. But I'm a good writer. I can sell stories to most of the big papers if I can back up my facts. I want scalps, Fitch, and I think you can help me get some."

"We're standing pat," George said, taking a swig from the bottle and handing it back, "My father is crippled. They shot him up so badly he can hardly talk and can't walk at all. Our neighbor down-creek has been shot in the last two days, and his daughter has been kidnapped. Otis Elliot is the front man for the railroad interests up on Sweetwater, and he was turned down by Em Graham several years ago. Now he has her.

"He also has a lapful of trouble, and he's just begun to know it. In the last two days we've messed up or killed about half the men he had on his place. Twenty-four hours ago, they attacked my mother's house, and we fought them off, then followed up-creek and laid an ambush for the second batch they were sending in. The marshal tells me Elliot's foreman, a big man named Sam Garvin, came into Solano yesterday and picked up another dozen men.

"We've got our work cut out. We can't hit Elliot's house while Em is there. So we must get her loose from him, keep him from finishing off our place, keep his men stirred up until they can't tell which way is up, then clear out the whole bunch. We have three able-bodied men, a seventy-year-old Injun, a crippled man, a good strong woman who can shoot the spots off a ladybug, and a little old Negress who does her best, even if she is eighty. Not to mention Sylvanus Graham, who is now so full of holes you could strain honey through him, and Lill, his Indian housekeeper. She's maybe sixty-five. Elliot's got maybe twenty, twenty-five men, with these new ones. We haven't been able to wait around and count casualties, so we don't know for sure how many we've put out of action."

Hastings's pasty face had taken on a warm flush, whether from the whiskey or excitement Fitch couldn't tell. "That's it!" he gasped, muffling his exuberance with both hands. "That's the story I've been wanting so badly I could taste it. I've sent in stories about old soldiers and children coming west to join their parents and Indian escapades, but this is the one I've been waiting for. Get busy, George, and tell me everything, right down to the number of buttons on Elliot's vest."

He whipped a notepad from under his pillow, took his pencil in hand, and George began to speak. He was impressed with the fact that Hastings double-checked every item, from the spellings of names to the exact time intervals of the various alarums and excursions. When he was through, the newsman ran his eye quickly over the scribbled pages. Then he looked up at George.

"I've got to be in on this. Can't miss it. But I've also got to get this on the wire. Can you wait on me?"

Fitch shook his head regretfully. "I've got to get back just as fast as Sunspur can make it, which won't be too fast at that. He's tired, now. But I ought to be there now. If I'd been twins, I'd never have left. I'll tell you how to find us, though, and you can come on when you can."

"That will have to do," said Hastings, taking a new sheet of paper where he wrote a careful account of the directions Fitch gave him.

"I'll get the telegrapher up, if I can bribe him to do it, and send off the story to my two top papers. Then I'll hire a horse and follow you. I just hope things wait for me to get there."

George stared at the small man across the pool of candlelight. "If nothing else, Mr. Hastings, make them sweat if they kill us all. We're either going to drive them all out of the Sweetwater, or we're going to die. Nothing in between. Just you be careful when you come. If they're on top, they won't know you from Adam, and they're not going to want witnesses. Don't get yourself killed on our account."

Hastings took off his glasses and wiped them carefully on his pillowcase. Then he set them on his insignificant nose and looked back at George. "Son," he said, "if there's a story in the middle of hell, I go to the middle of hell and write about what I see. I'll have enough on file, what with my telegraphed story and the one I'm going to write out and send by mail, so that if they do happen to kill me, it'll make an even bigger story out of what I already have. Instant confirmation, don't you see? For that, I'd not quarrel with the Angel of Death...not much, at least."

Fitch nodded. Then he peered out the window, and Hastings pinched out the flame of the candle. Nothing could be seen except black blurs, and nothing could be heard but insects scraping away in the grass of Ma Maloney's yard. George slipped through the window and stood on the grass outside.

"You know," he whispered sadly to Hastings as the window closed behind him, "when this is over, I'll have forgotten how to go and come through a regular door."

A faint chuckle answered him as he picked a cautious way through the squash vines.

Regaining his mount, he sent Sunspur loping toward the west. Another long night ride lay before him, and he was uneasy in his bones about the safety of those he had left behind. If Garvin had a fresh batch of men, he just might be intending to hit them again tonight. He could only pray that the lesson of that last attack hadn't been lost on the huge man. Surely they wouldn't try the same tactics again. And as long as Tracks was there, Fitch felt a certain security that he would foresee anything really out of the ordinary.

Now the patch of stars, which he had watched as he rode eastward, was halfway down the western sky. Sunspur had begun to lag, even with the frequent stops to dismount and lead him. Not many hours would find daylight upon them again, and Fitch wanted to be well into cover by then.

He should have been tired, himself. Even with the long rest his mother had insisted on, the night's ride was a killer, as he well knew before he set out. But something inside him was wound tight as a watch spring. A mixture of anticipation and dread held him in its grip, and he couldn't have slept if there had been time. The western line of blackness that marked the course of the Sweetwater pulled him toward it with such insistence that he felt he could run the distance on his own feet, leaving the stallion to follow as best he might.

It had been a long time since George had felt that particular sensation. It was a sort of before-the-battle feeling, and he knew that his instincts, honed to sharpness in that bitter war that had shaped him, were not deceived. The decisive battle of his own small war was before him.

He was more than glad to gain the shelter of the ridge just as a line of lighter sky marked the eastern horizon. He led Sunspur down through the trees, letting a low whistle go before them to warn any who were watching above the house. A dark form stepped from behind a tree and greeted him with a tap on the shoulder.

"Good to see you back. Do any good?" asked Herb's rumbling whisper.

"Not with the law...at least not active help. They're not going to look too closely at anything we do over here, though, and that's some comfort. And

I found a man who writes for the eastern newspapers. Let's go on down to the house, and I'll tell all about it." Fitch looked down toward the glimmer of light that marked the creek. "Any trouble?"

"Not a sign," Herb sighed. "Wasted a perfectly good night settin' under a bush when I could've been sawin' wood in that bunk of your ma's. Must be gettin' ole, George. Used to be I couldn't wait to git shed of houses an' women an' such. Now I kind of like my comfort. You reckon a man kin be ole at age thirty-five?"

"Herb, that's not old, that's sensible," Fitch murmured as they approached the house, signaled, and were admitted in one swift set of motions.

Kate, with her usual practical priorities, held off a discussion of George's trip until he had eaten and was sitting, stretched out, in his father's old rocker. Ab reclined on the settee, a shotgun at hand, with a more alert and eager expression on his seamed face than George had seen thus far. When Tildy came in with Tracks, whom she had brought from the barn, George told his story.

He told it to a collection of backs, for the listeners were posted at the windows and the front door, watching the creek and the slopes as the sun rose. Only Ab kept his eyes on his son, nodding eagerly as he spoke.

When George had finished speaking, Kate turned from the window to look at him. "It's more than I really expected. Throwing that writer into the pot is going to shake up the opposition mightily, too, when they get wind of it. The one thing they've had on their side is the fact that nobody really understands what they're doing to people. I have the feeling that even if we go down, they'll go with us. Good work, George."

Then Tracks came from the kitchen where he had been watching and listening. "Got feelin'," he said. "Better go quick, get girl. They do something today, mebbeso. We need all we get. You go get girl, I go get old man and old woman. Pink stay here to watch. Work fast, all right?"

Fitch looked into the squinted dark eyes, and he nodded. "Will do, Tracks Through the Air. At least, if we're all in the same area it'll be easier to keep up with what's happening to who. You can manage all right?"

"Take three horse. Make horse-litter, like see soldier do. Old woman help. We do it, mebbeso."

"Then Herb and I'll go see if we can prize Em loose from Otis and his crew. Maybe they won't expect us to hit in the light. We've been doing it to 'em in the dark. That Garvin...I hope he's so tired from his trip yesterday that he sleeps late."

"Garvin...bad medicine. Take care, Jorfitch. He see through big rock, you give him time."

Fitch thought of that as he led Outlaw to the ridge, followed by Herb with his mustang. As was his habit, George looked keenly up and down and across before stepping from the shelter of the trees into the rolling prairie land beyond. He froze in his tracks, and Herb, behind him, muttered, "Uh-oh!"

Garvin had finally thought of the free access provided by the high country that flanked the creek valley. Two men were in sight, one riding slowly on a long diagonal from northwest to southeast and one coming down the line of the ridge, some three hundred yards from the tree line.

Fitch and Herb faded back into the trees, mounted, rode at a good clip well down under the lip of the high ground toward the man who was approaching. A half mile brought them to a thickly wooded spot, and there they tied the horses in the bushes and concealed themselves beside them, holding their noses to keep them from whinnying a welcome to the third horse.

"Ought we to take him out?" asked Herb softly. "Seems a shame not to."

"Not with that other one on the horizon. He just might be keeping an eye on our friend here. They might be trying to draw us out so they can pick us off. We'll let him go on by. Then we'll tie the horses right here. They're just in our way when it comes to sneaking up on people. We'll go in on foot, taking advantage of every bit of cover there is. From what we saw the other night, there's a lot of stuff around Elliot's. We'll play it by ear."

It was almost another mile from the spot where they left the horses on the way to Elliot's. They took it fast, keeping high under the ridge in the thickest of the trees. Three men on guard went down as they moved, but not a sound marked their fall to George's deadly knife and Herb's powerful hands.

As they neared the stand of cottonwoods in which Elliot had built his home, Fitch paused and breathed in Herb's hairy ear, "If we get separated, I think we ought to head for home down the other ridge on the west. If they find the dead pickets, they'll think for sure we'll go back the way we cleared. Maybe those on the west will get pulled in if we make much noise about our business. Garvin scares me. He thinks too much."

Herb grunted. "Will do. Which-a-way we goin' in to get a look at the house?"

"I'm going around to slip in from the north. Not much up that way to guard against. You want to go with me or pick your own direction?"

"Well, I figured I'd mosey in right down the slope, here. When I taken out that guard, t'other night, I saw a right likely place to den up in, cozy as a squirrel nest. I'll git set, then wait for you to make your move. Then I'll liven things up from this side while you try to git the gal out."

Fitch punched him gently on the shoulder, turned, and slipped into the tangle of deadwood and briers that had been allowed to cover the hillside. He moved quietly, his old instincts rising up to take hold without conscious thought. The north face of the house came into view. Now that he saw it in daylight, Fitch realized that it was an ambitious structure for its time and place. Instead of the log cabin that others of the family had built, Elliot had hauled in lumber and built a big, square frame house. An upper story showed two windows toward the north, one toward the east. It was a good guess that Em would be up there where she could be more easily confined and guarded.

He lay in a thicket and studied the layout. The kitchen was obviously behind the door facing him. Its low roof projected further than the wall of the second story, and he wondered why Em hadn't found a way to slip out and down that handy way—until he realized that the windows above had been crudely but effectively barred with cross-hatched saplings, which had evidently been nailed firmly into the house itself. He could see two men on guard. One lounged just inside the kitchen door in a chair he had leaned back against a wall. The other was half concealed by the woodshed off to Fitch's right and halfway between him and the house. If the pattern held true, there would be two in the front area, also.

George drew a long breath. Then he set his knife between his teeth once again and wriggled into the tall grass that grew knee high all around the ill-kept yard and garden spot. He kept his eyes on his quarry, who stood in the shade of the woodshed, looking up the slope toward the east. He stood there exactly one minute and thirty seconds too long for his continued health and happiness.

CHAPTER ELEVEN

Fitch wiped his knife on the dead man's bandana. No sound had given any warning to those in the house, he felt certain, but he stood listening intently for a long moment. The position his quarry had chosen was all hidden from the watcher in the kitchen, which made it easy.

He heard nothing. Dropping again into the tall grass, he sneaked away still more to the right, heading for the shrubbery that flanked the house. Once in its cover, he rose to a crouch, for the spring weather had brought out a riot of foliage. He kept his head well beneath the level of the windows and moved silently along, straining every sense for a sign of the next guard.

Voices stopped him in his tracks. He was under one of the windows Elliot had strung all around the front of his mansion, and George figured it must be the parlor that was just above and behind him. He had never heard Elliot's voice, but he felt sure the peevish tenor must be his.

"I don't understand!" it was saying. "Everything was going so well. Nobody but my cousin and her clod of a husband was still in our way up here. How could things get out of hand so fast...unless you

146

made a mess of your end of things!" The last words were said in an accusing tone.

"And those men we sent west to watch the road to Santa Fe...why haven't we heard something? They've been gone for months, now. There's been mismanagement, and it isn't mine, you can rest assured of that."

George listened intently, feeling certain that the next voice he would hear would be that of Sam Garvin.

"Someone else has taken a hand in this game," said a well-modulated voice with British intonations.

George almost lost the next words in his amazement. He had heard that voice before. It was almost impossible to mistake it for any other once you'd heard its smooth baritone and its upper-class English accent. He focused his attention again on the man's words. He could remember where he'd heard it before when he had the time.

"Someone else has taken a hand in our game," repeated the voice. "You knew the old woman had sent a letter out to her son. You told me about Fitch. He was a most effective soldier. He has slipped through our watchers...or killed them...and is now here in the valley with us.

"We're faced with a mind used to combat. This is a man used to commanding men and doing it well. Make no mistake, even with the fresh men I brought in yesterday and even with the girl as a hostage, we may be in an untenable position."

"But damnit, I've done everything I could. I can't go out myself to bushwhack people...it isn't in my nature. Besides, that's your job. I understand that that was the reason the principals sent you to work with me. You're the specialist!"

The deeper voice hardened. Again George felt recognition sizzle along his nerves.

"You have my services because I was hired by those you serve to help you with this. They are my employers, not you. They do not trust you. I don't, either. I have endured you, asinine though you are, because it has been necessary to keep you quiet. We need this ranch as a base of operations. Now you are becoming a nuisance, and I tell you plainly that you will stop criticizing my work.

"If you keep your mouth shut, you may retain something of what was promised to you. Continue as you've been doing, and you will lose more than you would believe possible."

The silken threat of that voice made even George shiver. There came a stutter of words from Elliot, but George paid no attention to that.

He was remembering his trip to Tucson with a message for the marshal. He'd ridden through a blizzard to get there, and the deputy put him into the outer office to thaw out while he took the letter to the marshal himself.

Someone in another office was talking to a prisoner—this man, he'd swear on anything he could think of. That voice could not be mistaken for any other.

The interrogation had concerned itself with the disappearance of a gold shipment; he remembered that clearly. The deputy's twang had contrasted oddly with the cultured tones of the unseen prisoner. What he heard had roused George's curiosity, and he'd questioned the deputy who returned with a reply to his message.

"That's a real bad 'un, George," Williams had said. "He come to town about six months ago. Put money in the bank. Got cozy with everybody from the mayor to the bankers to the preacher. Got in with all the bigwigs. impressing 'em with his English ways, and he managed to find out all about the gold shipments.

"Come about, he set up a raid on the last 'un. Killed eleven men while he was at it. If Judge Bottle's maid hadn't took up with him and then got suspicious, we'd of lost him for sure. He figured she was just some sort of dummy for him to use and leave. But Ella's a smart girl. She caught on before it was quite too late.

"The gold's gone...took by his cronies, likely. But we got us one slick Britisher, and we intend to keep him."

What had that long-ago prisoner's name been? Fanshawe? No. Fenchurch! That was it! Sam Garvin was Fenchurch; he would have sworn to it. There was no doubt in George's mind that the voice was the same. Even the circumstances were reasonably close to the sort of thing that long-ago prisoner might do. He didn't remember hearing anything about the gold thief's escape, but if he had influential friends in high places, he had probably been pardoned.

If only he had known who Garvin really was! Hastings would have loved this angle, Fitch knew. He hoped the little newsman was on his way toward Sweetwater right now. Then he sighed, slipped downward a bit, and crept on toward the corner of the house.

Just before he reached it, he heard a cough. Freezing, he peered out through the leaves. The man

149

was settled into a clump of flowering bushes some six paces from the corner. He was evidently intent on doing his job, for his eyes wandered constantly up and down and across the yard, the lane leading to the gate and the house itself. He was doing it, George noted, to a set pattern.

That gave him what he needed. Patterns were the bane of white men. The Indians had had much success, simply because their own patterns were so much different from those the whites were used to. Fitch had worked hard at eradicating the need for that sort of thing. He waited until the man's eyes were turned to the southern sweep of his observations. Then he slithered out through the shrubbery, sank into the grass, and eeled across the space toward the watcher. Only a stifled gasp arose when he reached him, and one patch of pink blossom bloomed redder than before.

Now he had the entire western side of the house clear. If another man had been set there, he would surely have detected him during his movement from back to front. Fitch stared at the house from the shelter of his victim's bushes. There was a blind spot halfway between the parlor window and the two that probably lighted a bedroom at the back. The heavy stone chimney filled most of it, leaving a handy jagged slope up its height. In two minutes, George was climbing that miniature mountain. And in a minute more he was on the roof.

The shingles were still spongy from the snows of the past winter. Fitch's socked feet—he had his boots tied to the back of his belt—made no sound as he moved over the ridge toward the upstairs window above the kitchen. There he lay for a time, listening.

There was the sound of a solid blow against flesh. George started, then relaxed as Em's husky voice cried, "You touch me again, Mexican, and I'll tear your arm out by the roots!"

Without warning, Fitch pulled himself downward until his face hung upside down at the window. "Em!" he grunted, tapping at the glass, then cutting loose a part of the crossbars.

"Well, I'll be damned! George? You don't look like yourself, bottoms-up that way." Em didn't ask for instructions or wait for a reply. She hiked herself out of the window, looked around, tore off her ill-fitting skirt and stood there in a chemise, short petticoat, and frilled drawers. "Let's get out of here!" she muttered.

George grinned. He felt the thing spreading over his face, widely, foolishly, but there wasn't a thing he could do about it. Em had turned into a real beauty. She was still tanned. Her hair was pulled back within an inch of its life, as she had always worn it. Bruises marred the smoothness of her face. But she was that stubborn, fearless, determined girl he had known, and added to that was another dimension entirely. The bones of her face and body had grown into a graceful composition that nothing could diminish. She filled him with delight, even as he drew himself back up onto the upper roof and hauled on her hand to help her join him.

She sprang lightly up beside him, and he motioned to her to keep low and follow. They sped across the shingles toward the chimney, and she started down while he kept a close watch on the visible part of the yard. When he joined her in the shrubs, she put her mouth up close to his ear and whispered, "You have a match?"

He fumbled in his vest pocket and pulled out a sulfur match. She took it from his hand. There was much wiggling beside him, and he looked down to see that her petticoat was being stuffed under the edge of the house. She struck the match with much care and applied the flame to the flimsy material. It blazed nicely.

"Better go!" she whispered. They sped up the space by the side of the house. When Fitch dropped into the grass for his wriggling act, she observed, nodded, and followed suit, almost as quietly as he. They reached the woodshed with no mishap, and Fitch stopped beside the guard he had knifed there.

Em strapped the man's gun belt about her waist, drawing it into its last notch before it stopped trying to slip down over her hips. Then they hit the grass again, keeping the bulk of the shed as much as they could between themselves and the kitchen door. They reached the scrub beyond and paused to look back. A curl of smoke drifted out through the leaves beside the chimney. Fitch gave a sharp nod, and Em returned it. Then they hit for the slope toward the west.

"Didn't have to make any noise," Fitch panted as they scuttered through the low growth. "I hope Herb realized that and made it across. He's not the brightest thing in shoe leather, but he has a feel for this kind of thing."

They crossed the creek in a spatter of spray and ran up the slope beyond it. Behind them there was a yell of warning. Someone had likely spotted the fire under the house, he hoped. He'd just as soon they didn't yet realize that their captive had flown the coop.

They gained the ridge in less than a half hour. Turning southward, they followed the tree line, keeping a close watch for lookouts, as well as for Herb Yardley. They had gone almost a mile when Em touched Fitch's elbow and pointed downslope.

A large bulk was tucked into a brier patch, and George recognized Herb's creased and battered hat. "Herb!" he called quietly.

The big man rose smoothly from his hiding place and angled upslope to meet them. "Glad to see you, George. That was the slickest operation I ever didn't hear. How'n hell (scuse me, ma'am) did you get in an' out so slick? Time was goin' by, an' I couldn't hear nothin'. No shots, no screamin', no cussin'. Figured I better get my tail over here on the right side of the creek before you run off like an Injun an' lef' me. You looked back lately?"

Fitch turned and looked across the Sweetwater Valley, which at this spot was some three-quarters of a mile wide. A satisfying billow of smoke was rising from the spot where the house hid behind an arm of trees.

"A fine use for a petticoat," he said to Em, who was standing between the two men, her face somewhat flushed, but her poise determinedly unabashed.

"I heard once about two maiden ladies who burned to death, back East, rather than be rescued in their nightgowns," she said. "Made up my mind then and there that modesty is all right most of the time, but some circumstances make it ridiculous. Elliot took my dress away right after they brought me to the house. Thought that would stop me from escaping, I guess. That old skirt was stuffed back in under the bed, and I put it on to keep that Mexican bastard from staring at me so much."

They didn't look back again. It was terribly slow moving afoot. They knew that pursuit must surely follow them, but they did their best, and half the distance was covered when they heard hoofbeats behind them. They melted into what brush there was, Herb to right, George to left, Em scuttling ahead into another brier patch. Her white chemise was by now encrusted with enough grime and dead leaves to be inconspicuous, George noted with relief.

One horse, he thought, listening closely. Who? The hired hands would come in a bunch, he felt certain, if they thought they were on the trail of fugitives. Not Elliot, that was sure. Crouched behind a good-sized tree, he waited, watching the slope, the thin belt of trees, the cattle trail that meandered down toward the creek. Garvin's elephantine horse pounded into view.

There was no other in sight or hearing, so George stood and stepped out into the clear. His handgun hung carelessly from his right hand, but he didn't raise it as Garvin drew rein a hundred yards away.

The gigantic man dismounted a bit awkwardly. He held his hands in the open so no mistake could be made about the fact that he held no weapon. Without a word, he approached George's position. As he drew nearer, George could see that his face was still as expressionless as a boulder, but his colorless eyes glinted beneath his colorless brows.

"You Fitch?" he breathed as he drew to a halt some fifteen paces away. "Are you the man Kate Fitch sent for? Her son?"

"I am," George replied.

The man hmmmed deep in his throat. Then he began, "I am Sam...," but Fitch interrupted him. "I

154

know who you are. William McHenry Fenchurch. Late of His Majesty's Army, drummed out for conduct unbecoming an officer and a gentleman. Sometime investor in the Tombstone Bank. Now either escaped, pardoned, or paroled by a governor under the thumb of eastern interests. Also an agent for the railroad in their attempt to sew up all the land hereabouts. Correct?"

The big face didn't change. The eyes glinted a bit more brightly. "A man after my own heart. One who uses his head. One who might well make his fortune if he stopped to realize what could be done if he worked with, instead of against me."

"I might easily wind up hanging in your stead," agreed George. "When the election is over and some of your backers lose their pet congressmen, some fur is going to fly. Eck Margrave will see to it, once his hands are untied. You need a scapegoat, Fenchurch."

The man sighed sorrowfully. George stopped looking at his face and turned his glance toward the ham-like hands that were clasped loosely before him.

"Do consider," Garvin urged. "There are fortunes to be made here. Not in money...not at this juncture. But financial empires will rise from this activity."

"Not mine," Fitch returned, setting his heels as the hands tensed slightly. "You know you're covered, I hope? I wouldn't like for you to think you can jump me with any safety at all."

The hands relaxed. "Of course. Your beautiful companion. Otis was most annoyed at losing her. Did she accompany you in the nude? We found most of her clothing in her room. I had thought her too ladylike to go off into the unknown in such a state."

Fitch laughed. "If you're trying to rile me, you're going about it all wrong. Em and I have known each other most of our lives. Used to fight like sister and brother. She could come with me bare-ass naked, and it wouldn't make me turn a hair. You don't prey on your friends, Garvin. But you wouldn't know that, I suppose."

"Ahh. A young idealist. How charming!" Then the huge man sprang. Lithely, quickly as a panther, he was upon the much slighter man, and George found himself fighting for his life.

Two big hands wrapped themselves about his neck, and he punched madly at the face above him. Then he shifted his attack to the heavy torso that was helping the hands to force the breath from him. The world grew darker and darker, and his blows seemed to have no effect at all. Then, suddenly, the weight was lifted from him.

"Reckon you ought to pick on somebody your own size," Herb drawled, drawing back a fist and slamming it into the middle of the big face before him. Garvin's head was pushed sharply backward, but the man-killing blow didn't rock his balance. He caught Herb about the waist and lifted the big fellow off his feet. Herb set his teeth into Garvin's ear, and for the first time the giant yelled, loosing his grip and tearing at the trapper's head with both hands.

Fitch watched, his hand on his gun, unwilling to push himself into Herb's fight. Em shoved by him.

"We haven't time for such foolishness!" she said sharply as she jabbed the barrel of one of her pistols into Garvin's back and said, "Let go, Sam, or I'll cripple you for life. I'm no gentleman. You can either turn loose and get out, or you can lie here with a bullet in your spine. I don't much care which."

Something in the husky voice carried enough weight to make Garvin relax and spread his hands wide. Herb, realizing there was no resistance, loosened his teeth from the bedraggled ear and spat hugely.

"Now, ma'am, you jist busted up the first real fight I've had a chance at in a coon's age."

"There's plenty more where this one came from," she answered, whipping Garvin's gun belt from about his waist and tossing it to Fitch. "We've got more fish to fry. I don't even know if my pa's still alive. They're going to hit Fitch's soon as they get their troubles sorted out. We need everybody we have in good shape, not beaten to a pulp."

Garvin turned on his heel and walked toward his horse. The tension in his back showed that he wasn't quite certain that he wouldn't be back-shot. The three watched him mount and turn back toward the smoke where Elliot's house burned.

"We'll meet again," he said over his shoulder, and they looked at each other grimly. "I don't doubt it a bit," Fitch said. "Thanks, Em. You're right. There's no room for codes and such in a fight like this. We've got to get back to the house and figure out how to keep from getting killed."

Herb broke in with, "Your pa's all right, Miss Em. Leastways, he was when George here seen him. Old Tracks, our Injun medicine chief, is gone after him right now."

She looked up at the big man and laid her hand on his arm. "Thank you," she said. Then she picked

up the pace until both men found themselves stepping out at full speed.

Pink met them a bit farther on, leading Valley
and Sunspur. "We can ride double. It ain't fur now,"
he said, giving Em a boost onto Valley and turning
to climb onto Sunspur behind Herb. "Shore glad to
see you. We seen smoke up the way, an' Miss Kate,
she said, 'Git them horses over on the west ridge.
George'll come back that-a-way.' So I done it, an'
here you are."

So it was that mid-morning found them once
more in the shelter of the Fitch house. In less than
two hours, Tracks joined them, bringing Syl Graham and the old woman. Then Fitch went through
the house, counting noses.

"Three youngish men," he muttered to himself.
"Two women that can skin a live wildcat. One old
man who can shoot but not much else. One that can
hardly wiggle. Two old women that make up in
mean what they lack in size and strength. And one
genuine Cherokee medicine chief that can see the
future...sometimes. Damn! It's a mighty odd sort of
army. I just hope it's enough."

Kate, passing with a pan of slugs that she had
extracted from old Syl, turned an amused glance
toward her sole surviving son. "It's a whale of a lot
better than what I had to work with for two years,"
she said.

CHAPTER TWELVE

Once Pink had gone after Outlaw and Herb's mustang, and the entire batch of horses had been taken into the woods and picketed, Fitch dismissed the safety of their riding stock from his mind. From this point on, his sole purpose was that of safeguarding those who stood with him against the Elliot interests.

He called Tracks, Herb, Pink, his father, Em, and Kate into the kitchen for a conference. They sat on the long benches on either side of the sturdy board, cups of coffee steaming before them, and he looked down the row of sober faces.

"Garvin is a man so smart that he makes my skin crawl," he said. "Now he knows something about us...more than he did, anyway. We've hit the house twice, once by night and once by day. We've fought off a night attack here. He knows that we've used the nights to our advantage. I think he's going to change his tactics and hit us by day, right here, and probably this afternoon."

Old Tracks glanced up at him, his dark eyes squinted almost shut. With a nod, he said, "Mebbeso you right. Got feelin'. Something come, soon, mebbeso. You got plan?"

"It's going to sound crazy," George said. "Anybody in his right mind is going to want as much protection as he can get when he's attacked by superior forces in the light of day. And with two men disabled, not to mention the old ladies, it would seem totally insane to leave the strong log walls here. But that's what I think we should do. Let me tell you why, and what I think we should do. Then let me know what you think."

He talked for a long time while his listeners sipped their coffee and put in an occasional comment or query. When he fell silent at last, his father leaned forward in his chair at the head of the table and looked into his son's eyes.

"I'd never have thought of it," he said. "Nobody I know would've. But it's the smart thing to do. It'll throw 'em off their stride...and that's about the only thing we have...that's an advantage. I say let's do it. Now I know why they promoted you so...fast, during the war. At the time I thought...they must be short of officers, but I see that you've got...a real knack for this kind of thing. Take charge, general!"

Fitch grinned at him. Then he looked around the group again. "Anybody disagree?"

Herb chuckled, Pink grinned back, and Tracks grunted, "Better start quick."

Em and Kate were already on their feet, laying out ammunition in piles, checking weapons, putting together individual bags of jerky and corn pone. Once Tildy and Lill added their efforts to those of the others, it was less than a half hour until the tenants of the house were ready for their move. It wasn't easy, getting Syl up to his hiding place without showing too much activity. Fitch and Herb took him on the litter that Tracks had contrived for him,

160

and they spent an anxious hour moving through the thickest brush available, trying to keep from jarring their cargo, and keeping an eye out for unwanted observers. None appeared, however, and George hoped devoutly that Garvin was conserving every effort for his big push.

They stashed Syl under the overhang of rock that cropped out near the ridge. They had to remove a few rattlers first, but the old man assured them that any that tried to return would be sorry. Lill, who had accompanied them, took up her station in a notch around at the side of the rock, near enough to hear if her patient called but with a clear view of her field of fire. She was armed with the shotgun, as her rheumy old eyes were too dim for accurate rifle shooting.

Behind them came the rest, except for Ab. They flitted, one at a time, up varying parts of the slope, carrying weapons, ammunition, food bags, canteens, and even blankets, in case their vigil might last all night. George, watching from the top, was pleased to note that anyone not specifically watching for such a mass exodus would never have noticed their movements.

When all were in position, concealed behind logs, in abandoned badger holes, in thick clumps of trees, he nodded to Herb, and they set out down the hill after Ab, who had volunteered to watch until all were set. They found him at the western window, in his big chair.

"I think I saw movement on the west ridge a few minutes ago. Might have been a sniper getting into position. Might have been a lookout. We'd better be careful, general," he said, as George boosted him onto Herb's back, where was caught up piggyback by the big man.

Herb shifted him into a more comfortable position, then looked at George. "Might better go outen the back window agin," he said. "Iffen somebody's up there watchin'. We want to keep the house between us as long as we kin."

Once they were outside, they went over the same fence that had sheltered George before, following it toward the clump of trees where he had blown the concealed attackers away a couple of nights before. There an arm of trees came down very close to the yard, and they got down and helped Ab as he dragged his useless legs along with his elbows. There was no sound, no indication that any watcher might have detected their movements, and when they reached the heavy timber, Herb took up Ab again, and they made for the higher ground with all speed.

Behind them they left the stench of rotted flesh, for nobody had taken time or thought to scrape up the remains of those who had been killed among the trees. Fitch was glad when they were far enough away for the breeze to carry the smell off.

"Only difference between a big war and a little one is the big ones stink worse," he told Herb as the trapper sank onto his haunches to let Ab slip down beside the rock that sheltered Sylvanus Graham and old Lill.

"That's no lie. I quit soldierin' for no good reason that I could see. Now I look back, that could've been part of it. Set in the mud for a week, oncet, smellin' my best pard rot. He was over on t'other side of the creek, an' we couldn't even git down there for water...here, Old Timer. You jist set back there snug as a daisy. I'll put your rifle right here, an' your bag o' necessaries beside it." Herb settled Ab into a notch in the south side of the rock, laid his blanket so the crippled man could lean back into the curve of rock in some comfort.

"Don't worry about me," Ab said, turning his head so as to locate others in their hiding places. "Just point out where our folks are so I won't shoot anybody by mistake. I see Kate dug into the backside of that knoll down there, but the rest might be anyplace."

George knelt beside his father and pointed out the spots that held those of their people who were on the south side of the rock, which blocked his view of everything to the north. "Lill's around the other side of this same rock, Pa, and Syl's under it. If you need anything, just speak to Syl and he'll pass the word on. She volunteered to take care of both of you. Herb and I better get into position now. You can see Herb because he's setting up housekeeping on your side, and you'll watch him go. Take care, Pa." George tucked the blanket around his father's legs and gave him an awkward pat on the shoulder. Then he moved away around the rock, pausing to speak to Sylvanus and Lill as he passed.

He took up his watch from behind a fallen log. He had chosen the spot because it was high enough to give a pretty good view of the house and its western approaches. The sun crept over, above the treetops, and he set himself again in the mold the army had shaped. Wait and wait and wait some more. Deliberately, he relaxed from his toes to his scalp, resting his body, though his mind was squirreling in his skull.

The sun was less than a quarter down the western sky when he detected motion in the trees on the
other side of the creek. From his elevated position,
he could see a flicker of light-colored cloth between
patches of leaves. A hat stood out plainly for an instant against a boulder. He lay against the earth and
watched intently as a line of men took their concealed positions at the edge of the trees, a short gunshot from the house and about forty yards from the
creek.

Good thinking, he had to admit. He had no
doubt that Garvin was the author of the strategy he
saw unfolding below him. A line of snipers to cover
the cavalry charge, he felt certain. Perhaps others
were trying to infiltrate this side of the creek as
well. He wriggled out of his position and squirmed
along, well out of sight, to Tracks's burrow.

The old medicine man had selected a badger's
diggings. Improving on the original architecture, he
had dug out even more, making a slanting hole into
which he had backed. By raising his head a trifle, he
could see over the pile of dirt the badger had left.
Anyone coming at him from the rear would miss
him entirely.

George hissed softly, and the dirt-colored hat his
mother had dug out of a trunk for the old man
moved a fraction of an inch upward. "You come,"
whispered the gravelly voice.

"I think they just might try our stunt and try to
Injun across the creek. Just in case, I ought to slide
off down there and take a look. You think?" George
asked, flattening himself along a slight depression in
the scantily grassed soil.

"Mebbeso we both go," Tracks grunted, beginning to slip forward from his hole. "Take Injun to Injun right!"

"You up to it?" George asked.

"No need up. Down best. We go."

Fitch watched as the slight figure moved with a snake's ease, angling downslope and to their right. No sound followed it, and he gritted his teeth and went after the old man, determined not to be outdone. They passed close to Em's position, and went near enough to whisper his plan to her. Her eyes narrowed with concern, but she looked across the way down a narrow tunnel of clear space, nodded, and sank deeper into her position behind a small boulder.

It took quite a while. Before they were even with the north side of Kate's barn, the sound of hooves could be sensed through the ground beneath them. They froze where they were, listening. There was a crackle in the brush between them and the barn, and Tracks pinned him to his spot with a glance, then took off in that direction. George waited, listening.

He could hear breathing. Off to his right, away from the house. One person's breathing, he was sure, after listening closely. He eeled through the brush at an angle. When he felt he was close enough, he stopped, his head behind a tangle of briers, and waited. The breathing was coming straight toward him. He grinned, though he didn't realize it, in a teeth-clenched rictus of tension.

There was a rustle in the briers, and he saw the shape of a head and shoulders moving on the other side of the clump that hid him. His knife whicked softly, and the panting breath was still.

He listened again, but nothing moved, so he turned toward the spot where Tracks had left him. Before he reached it, he heard horses coming, slowly and carefully. He thought they were coming down the bed of the creek, and he once again congratulated Garvin wordlessly. Then he started as Tracks reached out from the grass and touched his arm.

"They come," he breathed. "We hit 'em from down here? No time get back up."

Fitch grunted agreement, and the two scuttered uphill to a point from which they could rake the northern and eastern parts of the yard with fire, commanding, as well, much of the approach from the creek. As they watched, fingers tense on their triggers, the shape of a horse loomed through the screen of windows.

"I hope Pink is close enough to do some damage with the rest of those bombs," Fitch gritted.

Then there was no time for anything. The attackers had spurred their mounts into a gallop up and across the shallow, pebbled bottom of the creek, and the line of men in the trees had begun to fire methodically at the house, evidently hoping to keep its defenders down long enough for the horsemen to reach its walls.

Tracks rose slightly and fired. One of the horsemen flung up his arms and fell into the creek. Fitch took out the next, but the rest were coming fast, and even the burst of fire from the slope above couldn't stop them. Once they were well in view, he concentrated on bringing down the three who carried blazing torches. Evidently Garvin believed in an eye for an eye. Two of the torchbearers went down limply and for good. The third hit the ground and began crawling back toward the creek.

Some sixth sense within George was quietly identifying, the firing from above. There was his mother's Winchester. His father's old Sharps, Herb's cobbled-up piece that could send a slug unbelievable distances. Pink's fine newfangled Winchester. Another one must be the rifle Em had taken from Mark Trant's store. Neither of the old women could reach the necessary distance with their shotguns, and Fitch reminded himself to head uphill if either of those sounded off. It would mean a direct threat to his father and Syl Graham.

Then he was firing steadily, alternating between the milling horsemen and the snipers, who revealed themselves often as they rose to take aim. And then there was, among the mounted men, a huge figure on a tremendous horse. Garvin, come to hold his people to their task.

He drew a bead, fired, but at the last minute another figure came between, and it was the one that fell. He cursed and wriggled away to his right as a spatter of slugs ripped through the brush that had hidden him. He and Tracks had both moved often since the real fighting had begun, and he could hear the Indian's new rifle firing toward the barn.

Again he caught a glimpse of Garvin, and he waited for a shot. His opportunity came when the rest of the men went forward again, leaving the big man clear for a moment. The rifle cracked, and Garvin surged backward over the rump of his unexcited mount. There was a splash of bright spray as he hit the creek. Fitch devoutly hoped that he was dead as he turned his attention to those who were now riding around the house, trying to get at those who were decimating their numbers from their positions up the slope.

He dropped three as they moved toward the house. Then half of them went out of sight around to the south, and the rest disappeared behind the barn. George Fitch hit for the ridge, running stooped in the brush and trees, but paying no heed to the occasional slug that sang through the leaves about him. Above him, he could hear a rapid patter of firing. The racket of horses charging through brush was to his right.

There was a stitch in his side, and his breath was coming hard by the time he reached a good spot just beneath Em's boulder. Just as he was getting a bead on one of the horsemen just below and to his left, there was a *Crrump!* of sound, and something sizzled through the branches of the tree above him. Good old Pink and his homegrown bombs!

"Try to keep 'em below us!" he cried as loudly as he could. A renewed burst of firing answered him, and the two shotguns had now joined the fray. That told him it was time to move again, and he crawfished up the slope, past Em's position. As he went by, he called, "Pull back, Em. We need to stay above if we can. I'm going to see about Pa and Syl right now."

Her rifle cracked a reply, and he went off at a slant toward the big outcrop. It wasn't easy to reload on the move, but he managed and found that he had only some fifteen rounds left for the long gun. Well, he'd worry about that when he was reduced to using the Colts.

"Pa, it's me. Lill, it's George Fitch. Don't shoot, I'm coming in."

He was squirming toward the rock when Lill's shotgun blasted right above him, and pellets sang like mosquitoes as they passed over his position. Behind him a horse screamed, and a man coughed once, as if his innards were coming out. Then Fitch was rolling under the rock where he found Syl Graham lying on his side, calmly picking off whomever he could see with one of the pistols he had been given for fending off rattlesnakes.

"Evenin', George," said the old man. "Ain't seen hide nor hair of snakes, but looks as if we've got other varmints come callin'."

Fitch looked at him. He was mostly bandages, but his blue eyes were bright with spirit, and his aim was very good. While George watched, he spotted two heads that had popped up over a bush down—slope.

"We've hit a mess of 'em, and if you an' the old Injun took out a few down there, we ought to have 'em down to handlin' size." He shifted his position, and a groan started in his throat. He squashed it firmly and said, "I watched you two go skittin' off. Good idea, too. They might've sneaked up on us unbeknownst, while we was watchin' the ones on horses. Now look off down there. Ain't a one of 'em still mounted. It wasn't real bright to ride uphill into entrenched gunfire. They must've took the bit in their teeth. I bet Garvin's fit to chew nails."

"If he's not dead," George said, squeezing off a shot at an exposed shoulder. "I think I hit him down in the creek. Didn't see him again, but that's no sign.

"Look there, Syl! Is that something white waving, down by that black rock?" Before the old man could answer, Ab's voice came around the corner of rock. "I think they're trying to surrender. Look down there!"

"I see it, Pa. Can you tell what the rest of 'em are doing from where you are?"

"They look to be trying to pull into a bunch. Can't see any long guns, but I can't tell about hand-guns. Man in the middle's the one wavin' the white cloth."

"I don't trust this bunch worth a hooting of owls," George said, rising to his elbows, then crawling out to hunker beside his father. "I'll stand up and see what I can get out of 'em, but don't anybody else budge. If Garvin's still alive down there, he's likely to charge us with whatever men were left in the woods."

It was a balmy spring afternoon. The sun was two-thirds of the way down. But Fitch felt a chilly breeze along his bones as he stood to his full height and looked down at the huddle of men below him. To one side of the bunch lay Kate, her rifle trained on them as firm as a rock. On the other, Herb stood behind a tree, a pistol in each hand. Something about the way he stood told George that he had been hit, but he wasn't wavering.

"You, down there!" he called. The man with the flag of truce (it was the sleeve of a shirt that had been white) stared at him across the distance between.

"If you want to stop this mess, throw out your handguns over to your right toward the big tree. Any rifles or knives or such better go, too. We're dug in all around you. You can't do yourselves any good by going on with it."

"We're done," the man said, and George could see that he was young. Not more than eighteen or twenty. Then he thought of what he had been and done at the same age and honed his caution. "Come out, one by one, around the bushes ahead of you. Then lie down just below this outcrop. Slow and easy. I wouldn't want anybody to get killed while he was surrendering."

A clatter of flung metal hit near Herb's tree. He didn't move, but just held his guns steady and watched the men intently. They started up the slope, skirting the bushes.

Something sounded an alarm in the back of George's mind. Some sound, vibration, something different. At the same time, something downslope caught his attention. He hit the dirt, rolled, and aimed his Colt down the slope.

"Get down!" he cried to the men still standing below him. At that moment, a burst of gunfire came zinging up the slope, knocking down two of the men who had been, a scant moment before, in the act of surrendering.

"God!" one of them shrieked. Garvin's incongruous voice burred out, "Nobody gives up when they work for me. At 'em, boys."

George could see a scant straggle of men lying belly down on the slope. Garvin's big body was obvious among them. He took aim once more. As he fired off the shot, he definitely heard hooves pounding down the ridge behind him.

Garvin gave a convulsive heave, then he went limp. A voice shouted, "Lay down your guns. Every one of you!"

George Fitch let his head drop into the dirt. It had been so close. So damn close. They'd almost won, against unimaginable odds. He felt a tear seep from the corner of his eye.

Chapter Thirteen

For a long moment, the world swam around Fitch. He was totally exhausted. Despair gripped him as he felt hands catch his shoulders and heave him upward. Shaking them off, he struggled, half blindly, to his feet.

The grinning face of Hastings danced before him, then steadied. "My God, George Fitch, I got here right in the nick of time! Came over that ridge back there with the marshal and his men, with shooting down ahead, just in time to see the big fellow lying down there shoot upward at you and you shoot back. What a story! I take it your folks are on top?" The little man was practically jumping up and down with excitement.

George looked around him. His people were coming out of their varied hidey-holes. Eck Margrave stood beside Ab, looking down and talking very fast. Seven deputies were moving among the Elliot men, herding them over to the spot where their horses were standing.

He answered Hastings absently as he counted noses. Two crippled old men, both seemingly lively as pups. Two wrinkled old women, likewise. His mother—he started toward her, shocked at the sight

172

of blood on her arm, running down into the folds of her skirt. She smiled and sat down beside Ab.

"Nothing to worry about, George. Went through the muscle, not the bone. I've treated enough gunshot wounds to know. Go check up on the others."

Trailed by Hastings, who seemed to be talking out his story to himself, George found Em sitting, quite pale and calm, behind a tree.

"I don't know how in the world you stood this kind of thing for three years, George," she said as he approached. "I find that I don't like killing people at all. Even monsters like those. My legs won't work. Would you mind helping me get over to my father?"

Fitch leaned over and took her hands. She came up easily, but she swayed a bit. Hastings hurried to her other side, and they turned back toward the rock where Ab and Syl were holding court. The clean scent of her hair was mixed with that of sweat and grass and dust. His mother's dress hung on her, but she still managed to look lovely.

George tightened his arm around her waist. "You suppose Mr. Syl would object if I came calling?" he asked.

"Considering that we'll probably be living right under your nose for a while, you may not want to. I'm not one of your hearts and flowers women, George."

"Never thought you were," he answered as they came up to the rock.

She sank down beside her father and took his hand. "You all right?" she asked, and he nodded, eyes twinkling.

"We got 'em, girl! Absolutely fought 'em to a standstill. Now they've messed up good and proper, the marshal needn't worry about political conse-

173

quences. He's got kidnapping against 'em, as well as enough cases of cold-blooded murder to bury 'em alive. The marshal was a witness, himself, when they shot down their own men."

He shifted uneasily and closed his eyes. "When can we go home, Daughter?" he asked in a far-off voice. "I want to lie in my own bed." Then he was asleep, his hand still clutching hers.

"He may want to go home," said Kate, "but until he heals up some, I think you ought to stay right at our house. You're not up to round-the-clock nursing right now, and neither is Lill."

"Oh, I already decided that was the thing to do, if you and your menfolks would have us," the girl said with a sidewise smile at George. "It'll save George a long ride, if nothing else."

George returned her smile, but his eyes were busy, sorting through the straggle of people who now stood in scattered groups on the slope. "I don't see Pink," he said. "And I don't see Tracks. I've got to get downhill and find 'em. I'll be back when I locate the two of 'em. Ma, get Em to look at that arm." Then he was gone, his attention so concentrated on the task at hand that he hardly noticed the deputies as he shouldered past.

Pink had been stationed behind a lightning-killed tree off to the south, some halfway down to the house. The bag, still containing a few lumps that were their homemade bombs, lay where he had chosen to make his stand. George got down on his face and let his eyes roam across the surface of the ground. Every hummock and log stood up noticeably as he scanned an arc. There was a bigger lump, long and thin, down toward the house, and he stood and walked toward it.

Pink had crawled into a tangle of vines and brush after he was hit. For a long moment, Fitch thought he was dead. He tore through the mess, making a path to the skinny man's side. Kneeling beside him, George thrust a hand into the bloody shirtfront. A weak throbbing was evident to his touch. He ripped the shirt aside to see a nasty hole high under the collarbone. It was bleeding freely, but there was no pumping of arterial blood, and George sighed with relief. He tore off his own vest and shirt, wadded the lighter material, and packed the wound with it.

Then, very carefully, he lifted the small man and carried him down to the house. Though the doors were pocked with slugs, and the window glass was broken all around, he scarcely noticed the damage. He took Pink into the parlor and laid him on Kate's narrow cot that she was used to resting on while keeping watch. The light was still strong in the sky, the sun just at the edge of the west ridge. He hoped to God that Eck had brought the doctor from Solano.

He pulled the light blanket over Pink, turned, and went toward the kitchen door. Tracks had been on the north side of the house. Probably he was somewhere on the other side of the barn. As Fitch passed the bit of broken plow that his father had hung from the eave for summoning far-strayed sons, he gave the rusty metal a whack with the big bolt that hung beside it. He knew that would bring Kate, post haste.

The scrub behind the barn held three groaning men and a corpse. Patiently, George ferried the wounded back to the house and laid them on the porch. But he was uneasy. He had seen no sign of

Tracks, though he knew that he must be somewhere nearby.

At last, able to think of nothing else to do, he went into the middle of the area he had searched and called out, "Tracks! Tracks Through the Air! Where are you? Make some sort of noise so I can locate you!"

As he stood waiting for some kind of answer, the night breeze came swirling down the creek valley. It chilled his bare shoulders. It seemed to sting his eyes, and he blinked them hard a couple of times.

A murmur of sound reached him. "George Fitch! George Fitch! Here."

Following it, he burrowed through scrub, heading up the hill much farther than he had thought to look. A slight motion caught his eye, and there was Tracks, half sitting in a nest of bushes. The coppery face looked more than ever like old, wrinkled leather. The eyes were sunk so far into their sockets that the barest of black gleams was visible.

"You hit bad?" George asked, kneeling beside him.

The old man's lined face was weary, his gaze dim. "I am going to die," said Tracks Through the Air. There was no trace of his broken English in that wheezing voice. He pronounced the words as precisely as did Kate, herself.

"There is a hole through my lungs. Neither your medicine nor mine can stop the bleeding. That is something that requires no strange talent to predict."

George sank onto his heels. He stared at the Indian in astonishment. "You old faker...making us think all this time that you can't talk good English!"

The old man chuckled, but the sound ended in a bubbling cough. "It is always best for an Indian to seem altogether like what people expect him to be. It becomes a habit. But long years ago, when we lived with the Fleming family in Louisiana, I was taught to speak correctly, to read and write...even to worship the white man's God." He choked silent, closed his eyes.

George patted his shoulder helplessly. The Cherokee opened his eyes again. "I tried to teach those things to my own people. They would not listen. They rejected all of them. With good reason, I have learned. The white man has little to offer us, except death."

"Except friendship," said George. He stared into the demon-mask face. "Could you really tell the future?'

The wrinkles grew deeper. "To some extent. Many times it was just common sense. Mostly it was a sort of intuition.

"I have always believed in my own medicine, George. One day your own people will stop thinking of it as pagan superstition and recognize it as the science of all living things on earth...as a single organism with many facets. But that's too...complicated...." The labored voice paused.

George lifted the light body in his arms and headed for the house. "This time you are going to be wrong," he said. "You got into this mess just because of me. I can't let you die for my folks and my problems. You may be weak from losing so much blood, but I'm sure Eck brought a doctor."

Tracks stirred. "The law? Finally came?"

"Just in time to see Garvin shoot down some of his own men who were trying to surrender. I suspect that things are going to begin straightening out around here, now we're rid of Garvin and almost all of Elliot's hands. I'd bet on it...a prediction of the future, Tracks."

Tracks's face wrinkled into its grin. "You got surprise comin', mebbeso," said Tracks Through the Air. That was his last prediction. The light body quivered and went slack. George felt the indefinable change that meant his friend was dead.

When he reached the house he found Tildy, Em, and a young doctor Eck had brought out under protest from Solano. They were all busy over Pincus Wills.

George paused in the light of the lamps that were focused on the wounded man. Pink looked deathly, his skin grayish, his eyes sunken. He still breathed, however.

"Who is that?" asked the doctor, glancing at the limp form in George's arms.

"One you won't have to bother with," said Fitch. "Another friend of ours. He's dead. I couldn't leave him out in the yard with the other bodies."

He turned into the hall leading to the four-bunk bedroom. As he passed his mother's door, she called out to him, "George! Is that Tracks?"

"Yes, Ma. He's gone. I thought I'd lay him out on the bunk he slept in, if that's all right with you."

She nodded, tears rising into her eyes. "Johno's best Sunday suit is in the trunk, under the window. I think it'll almost fit him. We'll bury him in that... dress him in it, George."

Now the tears were spilling over. "Johno would like that. We'll bury him in the family burying ground, along with Robin and the little girl John

Fitch lost. Tracks was a good friend. We owe him that much."

She lay fully dressed on top of the quilt covering the big four-poster that Ab had made for her wedding present. Ab himself had been put into the bed and was snoring heavily, exhausted with the strenuous activity of the day.

She reached over and laid her hand gently on the curve of his shoulder as she looked up at their son. "Tracks would rather it had been him than you, George," Kate said.

Fitch looked down at the withered bundle in his arms. He thought of the first time he had seen the old fellow, staked out in the clearing on the mountainside. Those bright monkey eyes, the withered face looking up calmly, waiting for him to come.

He knew his mother spoke the truth. He nodded and moved away down the hallway.

CHAPTER FOURTEEN

Once Eck Margrave and his hastily deputized men realized the extent of the destruction and injuries now filling the Sweetwater Valley, they busied themselves with burying the dead and helping to treat the living. Only by watching the buzzards as they circled in the spring sky did they manage to locate many of those who had been wounded and hid or crawled away to die.

Garvin, it turned out, had not troubled to gather up his dead after any of the skirmishes before that last one. There were dead men, as well as terribly wounded and neglected ones, hidden up and down the creek. George saw his kin taken care of. Pink was conscious and seemed likely to live. Herb was taking full charge of the small man, shooing away any of the women who tried to do any of the nursing.

"This little scoundrel'll drive you scatty," he said to Em when she tried to wash the patient. "I'll do him. I know how to keep him in line!" He glared at Pink, who tried to shrug and winced instead.

Those who weren't taking care of people were being taken care of. George, feeling secure about that, sought out Eck. "I'm going after Elliot," he told the marshal. "How much of a problem is it going to make if—when I catch up to him?"

Margrave gazed out over the creek from the porch where they stood. "Well, I'll tell you. After such a mess as this one, which I was not allowed to prevent, I feel that anything that takes place out of my sight hasn't happened at all. Just don't tell me about it, when you come back; don't even tell me if you found him or not. I don't want to know."

Outlaw was rested and well fed. George saddled him in the barn and rode down to the creek. Elliot would not be on this side of it, he was certain. He hadn't taken part in the attack. Nobody had found a trace of him after the battle, though Eck and his men had searched as well as they could take the time to do, with everything else that needed to be done.

Now George felt the need of Tracks. The old Indian might have had some intuition as to the direction taken by his quarry.

What had the old man said there at the end? A day would come when the white man would know the science of all living things—something like that. And George had always had hunches of his own, even before he met Tracks.

He couldn't search out all the miles of land around the Sweetwater, he knew. Perhaps he could have a hunch that would send him correctly. But how did you seek out a hunch? How did you court an intuition?

Far out on the grassland, George dismounted and ground-tethered Outlaw. He sat on the spring-green grass, gazing westward at the ragged edge of the horizon. He put everything out of his mind. Except for one thing, of course: Where would he have gone, if he had been Elliot, fleeing his just and certain punishment?

He thought of the land around the Sweetwater. He would not have gone east. Too many people. To the west there were mountains, water, if you knew where to look. Toward Trant's?

Not quite. Perhaps toward Coyote Creek. It would give both water and cover to anyone traveling toward the northwest. Suddenly, Fitch was filled with certainty.

He turned Outlaw's head to the west. Coyote Creek was as good a place to begin as any, and he had a feeling that he would find Cousin Otis somewhere along its wandering course. If not—then he was wrong, and that was simply that.

He traveled for two days, forging steadily along by day, camping without fire, usually, for a few hours of the night. He came to the fringe of trees along the creek on the morning of the third day.

He knew he had been right when a shot cracked among the trees, and his hat flew off. He hit the ground, rolled, and came up with his pistol drawn, to take cover behind a scrubby bush.

Outlaw had run off to a clump of stunted trees where he took cover with the innate good sense of a horse used to battle and sudden death. George let him be. He would stalk his quarry on foot. When he caught up with Otis—and he couldn't imagine that it was anyone else—the reckoning would satisfy some savage compulsion he hadn't known he was capable of feeling.

George flattened on the ground and snaked around the bush toward a big rock sticking up some ten yards farther on toward the creek. A shot puffed up dust just short of him as he went to cover behind it.

That had to be Elliot. He wasn't the sort to be a good shot, George figured. And this fellow was a rotten one.

Hatless, covered with dust, George Fitch stood slowly up from behind the rock. He started walking toward the shelter of the creek bank as deliberately as if out for a Sunday stroll.

"Fitch! Stop where you are! I'll shoot...see if I won't!" came the cry from the creek.

George said nothing. His boots made a steady rhythm against the soil as he neared the creek. Another shot lifted dust beside his right heel. Oblivious, he stepped forward. His pistol hung loosely in his hand. He didn't want to shoot the bastard. He wanted to strangle him, slowly, with both hands and a lot of pleasure.

Something of his attitude seemed to come through to the man in the creek bed. There was the sound of scrambling steps, a splash as if someone had run through water. Fitch picked up his pace and came to the spot where the ambusher had lain. A black coat lay across a bush. The remnants of a fire told of at least two nights' camping there.

"Elliot!" His voice seemed to echo among the straggle of trees. He stepped down, saw the prints in the edge of the soil leading into the water. The stony bed took no track, but another set led up the other side of Coyote Creek.

"Going up the country to the Taos Pass, eh Otis? Going to ground up in the rough country? Not quite. You might as well stop where you are. I'll keep coming on until I get you!"

Deadfall crackled somewhere up ahead. Fitch lost the false calm that had gripped him. Now he sprang forward like a cat after its prey, running lithely in the wake of the man he hunted. The thudding of his own feet and his heart hid the fact, for a moment, that the running feet ahead of him had stopped.

He came out into a small clearing surrounded by scrub and rocks. Elliot stood with his back against a slab of rock. He was panting hard, his shirt open at the neck. His gun was in his hand, but he didn't seem to notice it. He was staring at Fitch, his eyes wide and wild like those of a horse that was about to bolt.

"Give it up, Otis. We're going back to Solano to hang you. With or without the marshal's consent," said George.

"No!" The word was almost a scream. "I have money! I'll pay you to let me go!"

George lowered his gun and began to laugh. "Money?" he chortled. "You think money can buy you a way out of this? You've killed people left and right. Shot up my own pa. Run my folks out of their own places. Brought in madmen like Garvin. And you think you can *pay* me to let you go? I'm having a hell of a time keeping my hands off you, you know."

He caught his breath, calmed his mind. Coldly, he continued. "I want to strangle you, Otis. I want to see you plead and squirm and beg, and that is something I never thought I'd live to do. You have still another mark against you in my book—you made me almost act like the sort of vermin you are. Now drop that gun and come with me. It's a long way back to the Sweetwater."

The man's eyes went even wider, though Fitch wouldn't have thought it possible. The hand with the gun jerked up, and before Fitch could respond Otis Elliot had put a bullet into his own brain.

George stood there, stunned by the sudden end of his quest. He hadn't expected that. He had thought Elliot too cowardly to take his own life. He had been wrong.

"Well, old Tracks, what do you think about that?" he asked softly.

A little breeze curled about his shoulders, rippled Elliot's limp shirt, and wandered away up the creek. Fitch sighed.

His first impulse was to take the man home, but the thought of tainting the Fitch burying ground with his carcass made him sick. Should he bury him here? Why should he?

Otis and Garvin had left their own men to rot where they fell. The same was good enough for him.

George turned on his heel and went back to call Outlaw from his hiding place. Overhead, a buzzard was already circling, spiraling lower and lower toward the still shape beside the rock.

EPILOGUE

Nobody asked George about Elliot when he came back down the creek to his home. His mother looked into his eyes. A small smile touched her lips, and she turned away to tend to her cooking.

Em didn't ask anything, for which he was profoundly grateful. None of the others seemed to heed the fact that he had been gone for almost a week. He appreciated it a lot.

The place was getting back into shape rapidly. Margrave had sent materials for replacing windows and slug-riddled walls as soon as he returned to Solano. The doctor had left his patients on the road to recovery, taking with him the wounded from Garvin's group.

When George felt that things were in hand around his own home, he headed toward Trant's place. The old couple would be worrying, he knew. And Trant was delighted with the news George brought him. In addition, Mrs. Trant seemed to be gaining weight and strength with the coming of the warmer weather. Slowly but certainly, she was gaining on the sickness that had griped her. Mark Trant had hope, and George could only pray that it was true.

"We'll come over when we can find the time and help you get things into shape again," George told them. "We owe you a lot...you stood by Ma and Pa, and I'll never forget that."

He left for home with a lighter heart than he had carried for a long while. There was still a lot to do to repair the damage of the attacks the house had sustained. Fences were down, cattle scattered. There was enough work for ten men, and somehow it was satisfying to him.

Syl Graham, tough as the proverbial nut, was now able to recline in a chair in the sun to offer advice to the workers. George began replacing splintered shutters and shattered glass under his direction.

"Now, my son," the old man said, "was a master hand at anything around the house. Wish't I knew where he got off to. He's been gone over a year now."

George dropped his hammer. Filled with astonishment that he could have gone for so long without thinking to relieve the old man's mind, he said, "Mr. Syl, you're going to kill me!"

Graham cocked his grizzled head and said, "Now why should I shoot such a likely candidate for a son-in-law?"

"Because I've been so busy I've forgotten to tell you something. In all the confusion, I forgot about young Syl."

The old man started, then grew very still.

George went on "We found him, dead, right after we got here. Elliot's men had killed him and hung him in John Fitch's smokehouse." George sat on the edge of the porch beside the old man.

"I had to hide in there with him one evening, in fact. I don't know how I could have forgot! We'll go right down and get him and put him right next to Tracks."

Graham closed his faded eyes. When he opened them, he gave a long sigh.

"You can't know it, George, but you've comforted me. I had a feelin', way down in the bottom of my heart, where I couldn't get rid of it, that my son had run off and left his sister and me to fight it out with Elliot alone. I should've knowed better. I did know better. And now I don't have to live with that sneakin' little doubt any longer. Thank you, Son. Thank you."

So Young Syl was buried in the family plot, keeping Tracks company. There was more relief than grief in his funeral—to be missing is a much more worrisome thing than to be safely dead.

When things had settled down a bit, Em summoned George into the kitchen one morning. She had been making bread, and her arms were floury, her face flushed.

"George," she said, thumping her fist into a pile of elastic dough, "I'm a person who knows her own mind. I'm too old to take time for a lot of courting and such nonsense. I don't like that sort of thing, anyway. Let's get married and then get on with living."

Fitch doubled over with laughter. It came out of him in healthy whoops, bringing his mother, Herb, and both the old women on the run to find out what was happening.

"Put on your bonnets, ladies," Fitch laughed. "Spruce up, gentlemen. You're going to a wedding!"

188

There was not much surprise among his listeners. They'd all been expecting something of the sort for days.

"Tomorrow," said his mother firmly. "Let's not have it said that we had a hurry-up wedding!"

Before they could start off the next morning, Arthur Hastings came riding up astride a horse that seemed almost as uncomfortable to be under him as he seemed to be at being atop it.

"Fitch! Fitch!" he called, coming down the trail they had worn up the ridge. "Garvin was a wanted man! You were right...he was Fenchurch! The marshal sent inquiries through to the East. Not only was he wanted for the Tucson gold robbery, but he also had killed a prominent banker in Boston. It was one of the very men who helped him escape after the Tucson affair." He dismounted, walking as if his legs had turned to rubber.

The group, dressed in their wedding finery, looked at him. "What are you saying?" asked Fitch, his tone neutral.

"That there's a reward...a big one! Margrave sent a deposition that he saw you shoot the man he knew as Garvin, who was really Fenchurch. They're sending a draft to the bank in Santa Fe. You'll have enough to fix up all the things that bunch messed up, get some more cattle...most anything you want or need to do."

George reached out and hugged the astonished little man. "Mr. Hastings, you are hereby invited to my wedding!" he said.

The group started up the slope to the ridge that had been watered with so much blood. George, looking about, was thinking about a coppery face, grayed with approaching death.

189

FEUD AT SWEETWATER CREEK, BY ARDATH MAYHAR

"You got surprise comin', mebbeso," old Tracks Through the Air had said. Somewhere, George felt in his bones, the old man's demon-mask face was laughing heartily.

ABOUT THE AUTHOR

The author of sixty-two books, more than forty of them published commercially, **ARDATH MAYHAR** began her career in the early eighties with science fiction novels from Doubleday and TSR. Atheneum published several of her young adult and children's novels. Changing focus, she wrote westerns (as **Frank Cannon**) and mountain man novels (as **John Killdeer**). Four prehistoric Indian books under her own name came out from Berkley. Historical western *High Mountain Winter* was published by Berkley Books under the byline **Frances Hurst**.

Recently she has been working with on-line publishers. *A Road of Stars* was her first original novel to appear in print-on-demand format. Many of her out-of-print titles are now available from e-publishers fictionwise.com and renebooks.com; other novels are being reprinted via the Borgo Press Imprint of Wildside Press and Amazon.com.

Now in her seventies, Mayhar was widowed in 1999, after forty-one years of marriage, and has four grown sons. She now works at home, writing short fiction and nonfiction, and doing book doctoring professionally. Her web pages can be found at: w2.netdot.com/ardathm/ and http://ofearna.us/books/mayhar.html.